The Final Page of Baker Street

(In which are depicted the exploits of Mr. Sherlock Holmes, Dr. John H. Watson, and Master Raymond Chandler)

Edited By

Daniel D. Victor

Paperback ISBN 9781780927053
ePub ISBN 978-1-78092-706-0
PDF ISBN 978-1-78092-707-7

Published in the UK by MX Publishing
335 Princess Park Manor, Royal Drive,
London, N11 3GX
www.mxpublishing.co.uk
Cover design by www.staunch.com

Daniel D. Victor

Here's another one for Norma, Seth and Ethan

Acknowledgments

My deepest appreciation for their help goes to Calista Lucy, Dulwich College Archivist; to Mariusz Gasior, Access Team Librarian at the Imperial War Museum; to Chris Morton, Information Manager of The National Gallery; and to Roger Johnson, editor of The *Sherlock Holmes Journal*. On a more personal level, many thanks again to Barry Smolin, Sandy Cohen, Seth H. Victor, Ethan J. Victor, and Robert and Sylvia MacDowell. But the greatest thanks and love go to my wife, Norma Silverman, without whose inspiration—in more ways than I can count—this project would never have been conceived, let alone completed.

Chandler's time in London can be most accurately sensed in the writing of Arthur Conan Doyle. The . . . career of Sherlock Holmes spanned from 1887 to 1917 and captured a city that Chandler knew at first hand.

--Tom Hiney
Raymond Chandler: A Biography

In one sense, [Marlowe's world] is almost an elaborate transfiguration of that more simply and robustly cosy world in which Sherlock Holmes and Dr. Watson go about their familiar business, returning to 221b Baker Street for relaxation over a well-roasted partridge and a bottle of Burgundy.

--John Bayley
Introduction,
Collected Stories of Raymond Chandler

Editor's Preface

Dr. Watson never really understood whom he was describing. Oh, he knew well enough that he was detailing the story of a young man whom he and Sherlock Holmes had befriended as a boy. But due to Watson's death in 1929, the good doctor never got to learn that the youth he and Holmes had called "Billy the Page" would go on to become the famous American crime writer known to the world as Raymond Chandler. To give Watson his due, he did recognize the youth's embryonic talent. He even encouraged the boy's creative efforts. But Watson's mentoring wasn't enough to ignite Chandler's true genius. It would take a trip across the Atlantic, a home in Los Angeles, marriage to an older woman, and job-loss during the Depression to complete the transformation.

As a mystery fan who lives in LA, I've always been intrigued by Chandler, who set so much of his fiction in the "City of Angels." Reading *The Long Embrace,* Judith Freeman's insightful account of the time in LA spent by Ray and his wife Cissy, renewed my interest in the writer as well as a desire to discover more about him. My search took me to the Internet, a quick check of which informed me that there are two major archival collections of original Raymond Chandler papers: one, at the Bodleian Library in Oxford University, England; the other, at the Charles E. Young Research Library at UCLA. Since the latter is only a half-hour from my home, it was easy to choose which to visit.

Chandler would have appreciated my route. I drove west, following the curves of Sunset Boulevard, one of those "mean streets" Ray used to write about—past the Strip with its cheesy bars, rock clubs, flashy billboards, and swank hotels; through Beverly Hills with its sentry lines of ficus trees; and on to the university's research library, a large, square building hiding behind a bland façade of vertical and horizontal white strips. But as Chandler's stories testify, you can't let Southern California appearances fool you. Despite its unassuming architecture, the library houses a Special Collections room, which contains a trove of original works from all over the world. It also contained, as I was to discover, the typewritten manuscript of the book you now hold in your hands.

At the front desk of the Special Collections room, you request the material you want to examine. Minutes later, from behind a gilt Chinese folding-screen near the back wall, a librarian will wheel out a cartload of cardboard boxes. Like the files within them, these containers are all numbered, and you are allowed to take back to your seat only a single folder at a time. To protect the valuable collections, the lighting in the room is dimmed; but the tables are equipped with white-shaded reading lamps, so it's easy to examine whatever you've asked for.

And examine I did. Throughout that exciting afternoon, a wide assortment of Chandler-related writings and memorabilia paraded before me. Although they were encased in clear-plastic sleeves, I could hold actual letters to and from Ray, original photographs of Cissy, the entire typed manuscript of *The Little Sister*, complete editions of *Black Mask* magazine containing Chandler stories. I was so fascinated by the material that much of the afternoon was already gone by the time I realized that I had not yet looked into the largest of the boxes. Perhaps I had inadvertently saved best for last.

Oversized to accommodate full-length newspaper clippings, the box is about twenty-four inches wide, thirty-six inches long, and three inches deep. In it, large white folders, whose length and width are only slightly smaller than those of the box itself, cover the entire bottom. Since it's generally easier to open the large folders while they remain stacked within the low-walled box than spread-eagle them over the restricted table space, these particular folders had probably never been lifted out of their confines—at least, not the bottom one. Wanting to be thorough, I took all of them out.

It was underneath the last folder that I discovered the typed pages bound in twine that comprise the contents of this book. Though nobody seems to know how it got there, even if some clerk had at one time seen the manuscript, its title would have raised no concern. The innocuous word "Watson" is all that is scrawled across a yellowing top-sheet. Anyone who did come across the name would no doubt assume that some papers belonging to a "W" file had simply been stored in the wrong place. But since the manuscript was still there, obviously no such discovery had occurred. Until I came along. Curious, I untied the string that held the pages together and discovered this treasure—the heretofore-unknown history of the weighty relationship between Sherlock Holmes, the celebrated detective, and R.T. Chandler, a young student growing up in London at the start of the twentieth century.

I particularly wish to thank the directors of the Department of Special Collections at UCLA for allowing me editorial stewardship of the text. In that capacity, I have taken the liberty to add a traditional title and a brief afterword. To remind everyone of the fame that Chandler was destined to gain so many years after the conclusion of Watson's account, I have also inserted headnotes at the start of each chapter. Apologies made, I now proudly present to you all—readers, fans, students, and scholars—this most revealing tale: a narrative that helps delineate not only the psychological foundation of one of the great writers in the American canon, but also—if you read carefully enough—the shadowy origins of Phillip Marlowe, one of the most celebrated private detectives in literary fiction.

Daniel D. Victor, Ph.D.
Los Angeles, California
July 2014

An Introductory Word of Note

During the many years that I have recorded the adventures of my friend and colleague, Mr. Sherlock Holmes, I have had occasion to mention the pageboys, those young lads at our place of residence, who, under the direction of Mrs. Hudson, acted as servants helping to facilitate the smooth running of the household. To be sure, their appearances in Holmes' investigations were periodical at best. In the few investigations in which these boys actually participated, they generally served only to swell a scene or two or add embellishment to the backdrop; but the story that follows dramatizes a role of much greater significance. While my account describes the last few months that Sherlock Holmes spent in our old rooms, in reality, the focus of the narrative reveals the more complicated story of one of those pageboys— in fact, the very boy whom providence chose to designate the final page at 221b Baker Street.

As I hope my faithful readers recognize, it has always been my goal—as long as practicality and propriety have allowed—to maintain the highest integrity in reconstructing the cases of Sherlock Holmes. Yet one matter in particular has always seemed to call out for clarification, the authorship of a narrative that, despite its attribution to me, has for more than twenty years been continually questioned by the keenest of readers. While I have done my utmost to ignore the controversy, it is time for me to admit that such critical perseverance should be applauded. For it is only now, with the principal players who could have been harmed either gone from our shores or dead, that I am able to confirm in the following narrative those lingering suspicions about the first Sherlock Holmes adventure that neither he nor I, his faithful Boswell (or so he used to call me), had narrated. What's more, my deception precipitated a major and unforeseen consequence; for the callow writer who actually recounted the details wound up involving us in a much more significant case. How that young reporter found himself in our digs, how he came to write the story, and how his presence stimulated a further descent into the foetid and nefarious world of crime are all essential facts which the historical record has persistently demanded be made public.

Ironically, that story I *didn't* write had its roots in a trifling puzzle which I *did* report, a case that Holmes had resolved some eight years before. And while I myself did faithfully, if duplicitously, detail that earlier account, the narrative that follows will reveal some of the facts I felt compelled to obfuscate at that time. Although I will also provide the identity of the heretofore-unnamed chronicler, readers will recognise this revelation as a mere distraction, interesting in the long run only because its revelation helps illuminate the much more significant case in which that reporter later involved us, a case so encompassing that it threatened the very pinnacles of British society. Of even greater importance—and that which makes the account all the more fascinating—is that it dramatizes one of the most twisted and tragic stories that Sherlock Holmes and I ever encountered.

John H. Watson, M.D.
London, 1925

I

Show me a man or woman who cannot stand mysteries and I will show you
a fool, a clever fool—perhaps—but a fool just the same.
--Raymond Chandler
"Casual Notes on the Mystery
Novel"

At first glance, she seemed innocent enough, the dark-haired woman of middle age who came enquiring about her son.

On that cold Tuesday afternoon in April 1903, neither Sherlock Holmes nor I could possibly have anticipated the chain of events her visit would trigger so many years later, a chain of events that would not only ensnare us in a web of violence and murder, but also threaten the stability of one of the most powerful publishing empires in all of England. But that is exactly what happened. A seemingly insignificant episode of eight years past prompted the arrival at Baker Street of a client who would inadvertently entangle us in a tale much more complicated and ominous than the simple case she had originally come to discuss.

But I anticipate myself.

With a thick yellow fog blanketing London, a fire crackled in the hearth, and Sherlock Holmes, clad in his mouse-coloured dressing gown, was drawing aside the white muslin curtain at our bow window. It was the grating of wheels and the clatter of hoofs on the cobblestones below that had caught his attention.

"Like old times, eh, Watson?" he mused, wiping a circle of condensation from the leaden glass. "Perchance a new case to get the blood moving."

However enticing such a prospect might have been in my earlier life, I was by this time dwelling with my wife in Queen Anne Street and, despite the eerie fog, simply paying my old friend a visit. I was certainly not in the market for any new escapades; such adventures were no longer an option for an old married man like me. To the unencumbered Sherlock Holmes, of course, the game was forever afoot.

"As best I can make out through this muck," Holmes observed, "a woman of about forty years has just got out from a hansom cab, and she is now matching the house number against one written on some sort of card . . . . No, actually, on the back of a photograph."

Holmes let the curtain drop and, exchanging the dressing gown for his burgundy smoking jacket, remained standing for the few minutes it took Mrs. Hudson to usher into the sitting room the woman whom Holmes had described. With sharp features and luxuriant brown hair arranged in a chignon, she appeared quite the handsome caller—yet dressed in navy gabardine, also a traditional one. Her only *accoutrements* included a delicate silver watch-pin fastened with a tiny ribbon at the left of her heart and a small, black-beaded reticule whose gilt clasp she was continuously massaging with her right thumb. At the same time, her nervous blue eyes constantly surveyed the surroundings.

I rose to join Holmes in greeting her.

"Mrs. Florence Thornton Chandler," our landlady announced and quietly exited, closing the door behind her.

"Mrs. Chandler," Sherlock Holmes said, "allow me to introduce Dr. Watson, my colleague and associate. You may speak freely in front of him." Indicating the armchair opposite ours and nearest the fire, he added, "Pray take a seat and tell us what brings you here on so gloomy a day."

The woman nodded in my general direction and was proceeding toward the chair Holmes had offered when he added, "I can only wonder what you've come to talk to me about. That is, of course, besides the concern you have regarding your son at Dulwich College."

Mrs. Chandler stopped abruptly and turned to stare at my friend. It was exactly the kind of reaction I knew he had hoped to elicit. Despite Holmes' famed stoicism, he never failed to enjoy what appeared to others as a mystifying clairvoyance.

"Elementary, my dear Mrs. Chandler. Your watch-pin—"

"The ribbon, of course," the woman interrupted. Despite her unease, she managed a sheepish smile. Initially, she might have felt taken advantage of, but having displayed her own acumen, she could allow herself a degree of satisfaction.

"True," Holmes continued, "even in so small a strip as the fabric attached to your watch, one can clearly see the College bars of royal blue and black interrupted by light-blue stripes. But may I also draw to your attention the tiny bits of black clay and sawdust clinging to the edges of your boots. As I discovered during a case a number of years ago, such a mixture is peculiar to the athletic fields at Dulwich."

"Quite impressive, Mr. Holmes," the lady admitted. "But you also mentioned my son. May I ask what led you to *that* conclusion?" Despite her British name, the dancing lilt of Mrs. Chandler's words and the mellifluous roll of her r's suggested an Irish origin, slightly tempered by an American twang.

"Ah, Mrs. Chandler, the merest trifle. I observed your arrival through our window. Despite the fog, I could see you clutching a photograph. And while the air is not clear enough to have allowed me to distinguish the particulars, even from this distance a large, white Eton collar at the neck of a dark-clad figure is difficult to miss. I presume that the portrait in question now resides in your bag whose clasp you are so constantly massaging."

Mrs. Chandler immediately stopped the motion, but Holmes paid little notice. "No wedding ring on your finger excludes concern for a husband; the collar in the photograph suggests a youth at school; and thus your obvious anxiety—so readily apparent in the gripping of your bag—assures me that the subject in question must certainly be your son."

Begrudgingly, the lady nodded. Only then did she take the offered chair. Sitting upright before the leaping flames, she faced us both.

"Now, madam," I said in what I hoped was a more genial fashion than my friend's, "perhaps you can tell us the specifics of what has brought you here."

Mrs. Chandler took a deep breath and then another. In those few moments, she seemed to be weighing her words, as if asking herself one final time whether revealing her worries might actually be in her best interest.

"Dr. Watson," she said at last, "what has brought me here—as Mr. Holmes has already concluded—is concern for my son, the boy in the picture. Oh, I hope I don't sound like a foolish mother, Mr. Holmes, but I have come at the recommendation of my friend Mr. Bannister, a servant at Dulwich College, whom you may have cause to remember."

"Bannister," Holmes nodded, "yes, indeed. It was eight years ago—the very case I alluded to earlier in reference to the black clay and sawdust. Watson and I were staying in Dulwich at the time so I could complete my investigation of a property dispute. I had been researching the Early English charter granted to Edward Alleyn by King James in 1619 that established Dulwich College when we were distracted by an academic scandal. You will recall, Watson, that ugly episode related to charges of cheating in pursuit of the Fortescue Scholarship. The results of a Greek exam were in question."

"Thucydides," I confirmed. "Reported in the narrative I entitled 'The Adventure of the Three Students.' By implying that the story took place at a university like Oxford or Cambridge, I believe I successfully shielded the reputation of Dulwich College. It may not be as celebrated a public school as Eton, but whatever I could do to preserve its good name, I felt obliged to do."

"For which," Holmes said, "I am quite convinced, its headmaster, Mr. Gilkes, remains fully appreciative."

"To be certain, sir," our visitor agreed. "Mr. Bannister told me how pleased his superiors felt when you were able to save him and them from public humiliation. To this very day, everyone who'd been involved in that embarrassing incident remains in your debt. 'Sherlock Holmes is somebody to be counted on,' is how Mr. Bannister puts it."

One could well understand Bannister's appreciation although he had obviously not confessed to Mrs. Chandler his own compromising role in the story.

Holmes smiled briefly and reached for his old briar in the pipe rack on a nearby table. Filling the bowl with the black shag he stored in the Persian slipper, he asked Mrs. Chandler the nature of her current distress.

"As I have already said, Mr. Holmes, it is my son, Raymond, who has caused me to come here today." Once she mentioned the boy's name, her eyes began to moisten. Almost immediately, however, she composed herself. "Although I was born in Ireland, Ray was born in America—Chicago, to be precise. Not long after, Maurice, his miserable father, walked out on us, and Ray and I moved to Nebraska to spend time with my sister Grace and her family. Grace had come to America before I did. Though we shared a number of summers with them in Plattsmouth, it just wasn't a good situation for the boy—too much drinking by his uncles and all-around crookedness—so we went back to Ireland and my family in Waterford, the very people I'd hoped to escape when I left for America."

"Returning to your childhood home must have been a difficult decision," I suggested.

Mrs. Chandler allowed herself a smile. "A difficult decision indeed, Doctor! My mother can be quite the dictator. 'Tyrant' might be a better word."

"From the proverbial frying pan into the fire," I offered.

Mrs. Chandler nodded. "My mother was the main reason I followed my sister to America. I had to get out of that house with all the bullying and snobbery and prejudice."

"But now you're here in England," I observed.

Mrs. Chandler laughed. "Yes. After leaving Waterford, Ray and I moved to Dulwich. We lived in a large, detached house called Whitefield Lodge in Alleyn Park just next to the school's playing field. In fact, it's owned by my brother Ernest—a business investment, I should imagine. He's a solicitor. My mother and sister Ethel were also living there when we arrived."

"So, still with your mother," Holmes said, exhaling as he spoke.

"At least we were free of Waterford," she explained. "And who knows? Maybe Ernest was happy to be rid of us as well. He too felt the hand of the tyrant. Becoming a solicitor to maintain the family law firm was not *his* choice; it was our mother's. Maybe he was even sympathetic. I must say that he's been most generous in agreeing to pay for Ray's entire education at the College."

"Very generous indeed," I said.

"And where are you living now?" Holmes asked.

"Since February of 1901, the family have been staying in Auckland Road in Upper Norwood. In a tall, red-brick house called Mt. Cyra."

"Most genteel," I noted as blue smoke from Holmes' pipe began to cloud the room.

"I do still visit friends in Dulwich," she continued. "Like Mr. Bannister. I suppose the black clay comes from the shortcuts I take across the playing fields."

"And the lad?" I asked. "How old is he now? How is he progressing?"

"Ray's fifteen," she answered, "and just switched to studying the classics. He's a diligent worker, but it's all new for him, and he's struggling to catch up." She paused for a moment as if she herself was shouldering her son's burdens. When she resumed, she had changed the topic. "I must say that Ray's doing well on the pitches. At this time of year it's cricket. He's a bowler. And in the autumn it's rugby. He actually broke his nose in a match."

"Good show," I exclaimed, having played some rugby for Blackheath myself.

"Obviously, Dr. Watson, it's not his athletics I'm concerned with. I don't reckon he'll ever be on the school's team or win his blues. No, I'm worried about whatever it is that's distracting him from his studies."

"A mother's constant worry," I said, noting how the melancholy had returned to her eyes.

"To be sure," she agreed. "And yet it's more than just his studies. There's an unhappiness that accompanies the boy. Perhaps it's due to having no permanent home—or father, for that matter, though how much good that no-account would have done is anyone's guess. Ray has strong opinions and few friends. Not only is he shy, but he's a day-boy, you see. Because we live so close to the College. Coming home to his family every night cuts him off from his mates. And then there's his American background. He doesn't know yet whether he's a Brit or a Yank."

"Neither fish nor fowl," I lamented.

"Exactly, Dr. Watson," said Mrs. Chandler. "But what concerns me even more is that during this last fortnight, Ray's been failing to return home after his rugger practices. He disappears each evening and then comes tiptoeing back into the house close to midnight. When I ask him what he's been up to or where he's gone, he just shrugs and goes off to bed. I have come to you, Mr. Holmes, to enlist your help in finding out where he takes himself every night."

"Perhaps," I suggested, "he's reading in the library."

"The library," she scoffed. "If he was gone studying, why could he not tell me, I'd like to know?"

Sherlock Holmes, who had been quietly smoking during this exchange, now spoke up. "More likely, spending time with some young lady, I should judge." Arching his eyebrows, he added, "Your son is, after all, a young man of appropriate age."

Mrs. Chandler sat up even straighter. "Oh, no, gentlemen. We may be lapsed Quakers, but my Ray is a good boy. He wouldn't wander off with some strange girl from the village."

Holmes expelled a cloud of pent up smoke. It seemed almost as murky indoors as out.

"Mrs. Chandler," he said definitively, "my line of work takes me into the criminal world, not to some Never-Never Land full of missing boys. I'm sure the police aren't interested either; it's not as if he's disappeared. You yourself might try following him or hiring someone on your own to look into the matter."

"'*Hiring* someone'?" she repeated shrilly, her nostrils flaring. "'*Hiring* someone'? That's why I've come to see *you*,

Mr. Holmes, isn't it?" She enunciated this last interrogative as if it were a statement. "I've crossed my husband and my mother to raise that boy, and I'm not about to be nay-sayed by *you*."

The set of Holmes' jaw revealed just how hard he was biting on the stem of the briar.

"As for following him myself," Mrs. Chandler went on, "I've tried—and been unable to keep up. Ray is, after all, a healthy fifteen-year-old boy."

"'Healthy,'" Holmes repeated disdainfully, yet obviously pleased that Mrs. Chandler's word had so clearly confirmed his previous point. His was an off-putting tone, as if he couldn't be bothered by so trifling a mystery despite the great concern it was causing the woman before us.

With his arms folded like a great brooding bird encased in long, feathered wings, Holmes sat motionless. A moment later he resumed puffing billows of blue smoke into the air. For her part, Mrs. Chandler once more took up massaging the clasp of her bag.

"Holmes," I found myself urging, "for the sake of old Bannister's high regard, you must help this lady."

Unmoved, Holmes continued to smoke.

"Holmes," I tried once more. "For the sake of a desperate woman—oh, bother, Holmes—for the sake of a desperate *mother*, you must bend to Mrs. Chandler's entreaties."

His silence continued for another minute. He appeared to be deep in thought. Investigating the activities of children was not his usual line of work. On the other hand, the woman before him seemed desperate enough to warrant his help. At last, following a sharp glance in my direction and a defiant final exhalation of smoke, he stood.

"Oh, very well, Mrs. Chandler," he said without an apparent ounce of sympathy. "As I have no significant criminal cases pending at the moment, even so trivial a matter as a disappearing boy should provide me with some cerebral activity. I shall meet you in Dulwich tomorrow evening at 6:00."

The lady grasped Holmes' hands. "Oh, thank you, Mr. Holmes, thank you. I am ever so grateful."

Sherlock Holmes displayed one of his more sceptical smiles. "That is your opinion *today*, Madam, but if I am any judge of the behaviour of adolescent boys, I fear your son may be up to the kind of activities you would prefer not knowing anything about."

Holmes arranged a place for their meeting the next day and then handed Mrs. Chandler off to me to escort to the door.

Once the lady had left, I offered my opinion. "A good decision, Holmes."

"I hope so, Watson. But to judge from the boy's secretive nature, as well as from Mrs. Chandler's exaggerated concerns, I fear that there might be more thorny issues brewing between mother and son than a simple accounting of his nocturnal whereabouts will settle."

Ω

It was not until the weekend that I could return to Baker Street to find out the results of Holmes' investigation. When I did see my friend again, it was Sunday afternoon, and I was just in time for tea. The fire was blazing, and Mrs. Hudson had already set our table. Except for an unfamiliar little bell made of cut-crystal that stood next to the white teapot, the nostalgic scene might have taken place some ten years before.

Holmes filled our respective cups with tea; and while I dined on watercress sandwiches, he gave me a full account of his adventure in Dulwich.

"The train was punctual," he began, "and with the fog diminishing, Mrs. Chandler and I met in the early evening— just as we had agreed—beneath the Italianate clock tower at the College. I'm sure you'll remember that *palazzo*, Watson. There's also a new library just built. It is a tribute to the Old Alleynians who died in the Boer War."

"Much of the school was designed by Sir Charles Barry," I seemed to remember, "the architect of the Houses of Parliament."

It was easy to recall the picturesque grounds of the college—the graceful structures of red-and-white brick, the large swaths of lush, green lawn, the armies of stately chestnut trees. I have always found that such pastoral beauty aids the acquisition of knowledge. Even with my own schooling in London—"

Reality interrupted my reverie.

"His son, old fellow," Sherlock Holmes was informing me. "Charles Barry, *Junior*, was the architect of Dulwich College."

"It's still a beautiful place," I responded weakly. No one likes being corrected, even by a man with Holmes' reputation for accuracy.

Oblivious to my embarrassment, Holmes simply cleared his throat and resumed his narration: "Mrs. Chandler escorted me to the athletic field where we concealed ourselves behind a hedgerow. From this hide, she pointed out her son, a middle-sized, athletic-looking lad with dark hair and brooding eyes. As I watched him racing his mates across the pitch, she placed her arm on mine and, giving it a supportive squeeze, silently waved good-bye and, as we had earlier planned, retreated to her home. I was left standing there to see where the boy might be off to.

"Fortunately, I had not long to wait. It soon grew dark and some wisps of fog hovered above the grass, but I could still distinguish the black suits and white collars of the young boys exiting the changing rooms. Almost immediately one parted from the group, shouting something about seeing them on the morrow. It was Raymond, of course. When the others had gone, he broke into a kind of canter, and I followed him at a distance even as he loped across the lawn. He continued up a hillock and finally down among a grove of leafy oaks, arriving at a small, square, wooden outbuilding not far from the gymnasium. He'd given me quite a run actually. With his galloping gait, it's easy to see why his mother couldn't keep up with him. If truth be told, old fellow, it wasn't so simple for me either."

I chuckled in sympathy. "Didn't Oscar Wilde have something to say about the shame of wasting youth on the young?"

"I believe you'll find that most people attribute the sentiment to Bernard Shaw," Holmes said. How much my friend knew about literature never failed to amaze me, especially in light of how often he claimed to be ignorant of the subject. His knowledge of literature, I had once described as "nil".

"But they're both Irish," he added. "You got that part correct."

Unable to discern whether I'd just been complimented or ridiculed, I silently watched Holmes sip his tea. He took a moment to enjoy the brew, then replaced his cup and continued his account: "I followed the boy to the outbuilding. Had I not been trailing behind him, I might well have missed it in the darkness. The building, a small square structure with darkened windows on each wall, is shielded from pedestrian traffic by the oak trees. Taking cover behind a broad trunk within the grove, I could just make out young Chandler creeping towards one of the windows.

"It had grown quite dark by then, but the fog was thin enough to allow me to distinguish what was happening. On closer inspection, I could see that broken lines of light framed the glass of each casement. It seemed obvious to me that someone on the inside had done his best to cover the windows with dark paper to conceal what was going on within. But his best was not good enough, Watson. The tell-tale light emitted at the edges of each large pane revealed the amateurish skill of whoever had attached the paper to the glass. Quietly, I stole up to a window on the side opposite Raymond to witness for myself what had been attracting the young man to this spot."

"And," I asked Holmes between bites of a chocolate biscuit, "what did you see?"

"It was a make-do photography studio, Watson, complete with lights, camera, photographer and model."

"Only a photography studio? One wouldn't need paper to cover the windows at night. Why would someone go to these extravagant lengths to conceal such a place?"

"Use your imagination, man!" he scolded. "What kind of photographic activity do you expect would draw a male adolescent to its windows every night?"

"I cannot imagine, Holmes—especially not at a public school like Dulwich."

Holmes smiled. "In fact, old fellow, it was actually a Dulwich student responsible for the scene: a young artist seeking to earn extra money had found himself a voluptuous young maid from town willing to pose for him. 'Carmen' is her name, a recent arrival from Spain, who needed money to send home to her family."

I dabbed at my lips with a linen handkerchief. "Proceed," I said drily. "I fail to see the entire picture."

"Ah, Watson," Holmes sighed as he leaned back, "it was exactly that 'entire picture' that Raymond himself was trying to see. But clearly, you need everything spelled out. Imagine." He held up his hands as if to frame a photograph for me. "The compliant young woman in question is sitting in a high-backed chair made of teakwood. For some artistic reason, she is posed on an orange-coloured shawl fringed in white. Although she is positioned rigidly with her hands on the arms of the chair, her back straight, and her knees decorously pressed together, she manages—with her white teeth quite apparent between her parted red lips—to present a smile that I'm sure some men might call provocative."

"But what was she wearing?" I asked. "Surely, it is quite unlike you, Holmes, to leave out the most obvious part of the description. Must I always have to rely on my own imagination?"

Holmes dropped his arms in exasperation. "Oh, Watson," he chuckled, "you do fail to understand. She was quite naked—well-endowed, and quite naked indeed."

I gasped in disbelief. When I could finally catch my breath, I said, "Surely, Holmes, you exaggerate."

"Pray, forgive me," he said, eyes twinkling. "I did neglect one detail. She was, in fact, wearing long, green earrings, possibly jade or *faux Fei Tsui*."

"Holmes, really!" I moved my plate away, no longer able to enjoy my repast.

"What's more," he continued, "to judge from the jerking movement of the boy's right hand—his back was to me, remember—what had attracted a healthy young male to the windows of this studio every night should be quite obvious. Especially a young male suppressed by Mr. Gilkes' stringent code of morality at school and by his mother's strict rules of propriety at home."

"Quite the expert in psychology now, eh, Holmes?"

"Certainly not in psychology, Watson; but I will say that, even though I am also no expert in matters related to the female form, the young woman in question had quite beautiful features. Small in stature, to be sure, but bare breasts shimmering like pearl in the bright lights surrounding her."

"Holmes!" I cried. "You go too far."

"Mark my words, Watson. It is not an image easily forgotten—even if one were so inclined, which I am quite sure that young Raymond Chandler is not. Indeed, I suspect that the boy will retain the striking picture in his mind for many a year."

I merely shook my head.

"On Thursday night," Holmes continued, as if I had registered no outrage at all, "I persuaded a local constable to join me; and armed with a mackintosh to cover the young lady, he broke up the photography session, removing both participants to the local magistrate. I imagine that paying some sort of fine should cure the two of them of their Bohemian behaviour. At least, for now."

"And young Chandler?"

"How curious you should ask. For while the policeman was performing his gallant duties, I found the boy outside still manning his position at the window. Even after the licentiousness had evolved into a simple police matter—the rounding up and arresting of the two culprits—those procedures seemed to fascinate him as well."

"Go on," I said, fascinated and repelled at the same time.

"I introduced myself to the lad, explaining that I was in the employ of his mother. At first he was quite incorrigible. He even denied his self-gratification; I imagine that he always will. But when he tried to bolt, I grabbed his arm. He kept trying to shake me off, but at last I managed to flag a hansom; and after a short, silent journey to Auckland Road, I was able to reunite the discomfited boy with his mother. I refused any remuneration, of course, and I explained to Mrs. Chandler in only the most general of terms what had happened. Actually, I told her that her son had been engaged in some school-wide pranks; and that while they were generally harmless, I nonetheless suggested that she consign young Raymond's free time to some more useful activity—perhaps in a trade or job of some sort."

"Well done, Holmes," I applauded. "At least, you spared a distressed mother the anguish of learning how low her disreputable son had fallen. Another case completed. I'm sure Mr. Bannister at the College will hear of your success as well."

Only after I had registered this approval did I feel at ease enough to mop my perspiring brow with my serviette, sample a final biscuit, and make ready to depart. It was time I left for Queen Anne Street and my wife.

Sensing my intention, Holmes made a request. "Before you leave, do be a good fellow and be so kind as to ring that bell." As he spoke, he pointed to the unfamiliar piece of crystal sitting next to the teapot.

"Waterford!" I exclaimed, observing more closely the iridescent sparkles that flashed from the gracefully cut facets. "That's not like you, Holmes."

"A gift from Mrs. Chandler," he explained, "she'd brought it from Ireland. But here at Baker Street it's become a newly instituted requirement—as you are about to see."

With a mischievous smile, he again pointed to the bell.

I arched a sceptical eyebrow, but lifted the dainty instrument and tipped it back and forth. No sooner did the charming little ring dance through the air than I heard the tattoo of rapid footfalls ascending the seventeen steps to Holmes' sitting room. *Whose?* I wondered; they were much too quick to belong to Mrs. Hudson.

The mystery of their ownership was immediately solved by the appearance at the door of a young man of medium height dressed in burgundy livery. He stood at attention looking very serious, his shining hazel eyes, however, unable to conceal his anticipation. With his thick dark hair combed straight back from his broad brow, he had a handsome, angular face marred only by a slightly misshapen nose that afforded him a kind of toughness.

"Dr. Watson," Holmes said formally, "may I present to you Mrs. Hudson's newest page. For the small sum she pays him, he comes up from Dulwich by train on his free afternoons and spends much of the weekend with us here at Baker Street."

My mouth dropped open. It was Peeping Tom himself, now obviously an attendant to our long-suffering landlady. Holmes had suggested that the boy's mother should secure him a trade or a job, yet it was obvious that Holmes himself was the one responsible for getting the young rogue this position.

"Student number 5724," Holmes said. "Master R.T. Chandler."

I was about to nod in his direction when the boy had the cheek to announce: "As I've already told you, Mr. Holmes, I prefer the American way of saying names—just 'Raymond.'" He spoke in an accent more flat than British.

"And as I have already told *you*," Holmes countered, "your preference doesn't matter. Here at 221 we call *all* the pages 'Billy.'"

"Ah, yes," the boy said, "just like back in America, calling all the Negro train-porters 'George.' After George Pullman, the inventor of the sleeping car."

"You don't say," I replied.

Daniel D. Victor

"I *do* say," he shot back. "My father worked on the railroad. He never told me much, but he did tell me that—before the swine walked out on my mum and me."

Despite the boy's gruffness, I was impressed by his interest in the nickname's origin. As a self-proclaimed wordsmith, I thought I sensed a kindred spirit. After all, one's sensitivity to language says worlds about a person's good character. Maybe the young man *could* be saved. If Holmes saw value in the lad, so should I.

"Stay interested in words," I advised the boy, "and your appreciation will stand you in good stead."

"Thank you," the boy now known as Billy replied. He seemed to be contemplating his options. From Holmes' account I knew of his recalcitrance, but obviously the youth could modulate his disposition. Suddenly, with a bright smile he added, "Coming from a distinguished author like yourself, Dr. Watson, such a compliment means the world to me."

"Much obliged, my lad," I said. The boy knew how to charm; there was no doubt about that. One could see how a timely grin had brightened his face. Yet even now, as his lips maintained a serviceable smile, I could detect in the shadows surrounding his eyes the gloom of which his mother had spoken. She had called him shy; but with his misshapen nose and expressive mouth, "troubled" might be a more accurate term. Certainly, within this young man were waters that ran deep.

Seeing him standing so close to Holmes, I could only imagine what melancholy effects the two of them might have on each other. Due to my recent marriage, Holmes had been deprived of his usual long-time companion. Thanks to

Holmes' detective work, Billy had been deprived of his nocturnal adventures. *Might two negatives equal a positive?* I wondered. One could only guess.

Thinking of my marriage reminded me once again that it was time to return home to my wife. I exchanged farewells with Holmes and took my derby from young Billy. I smiled again at the lad and made my way downstairs and through the front door. Once outside in the cold air, I was greeted by a cacophony of honks, shouts, cries, and whinnies—all of which welcomed me back to the hurly-burly of Baker Street in which I felt so comfortable. For Holmes' sake, I hoped the newcomer would feel the same.

II

A good story cannot be devised; it has to be distilled.
--Raymond Chandler
Letter to Mrs. Robert Horgan

I visited Holmes only sparingly in the spring of 1903, but Billy's arrival assuaged my guilt. Marital bliss and a successful surgery preoccupied me although I must confess that on the few occasions I did manage to see my friend, I sensed a longing in both of us for the close companionship we had enjoyed for so many years in our adventures together. But I had my home life and medical patients to attend to; Holmes, no matter how intriguing some case here or there might be, still had only his solitary digs to return to. And I well knew that, with nothing challenging to entertain his active brain, Sherlock Holmes could easily fall back on self-destructive means to divert his attention.

For just that reason, when Holmes was on his own in those days following my marriage, I was always happy to encounter Billy the page. Despite the repugnant manner in which Billy had first made Holmes' acquaintance, the boy created a most positive impression once he began his duties. Whenever he had free moments at school, he would travel to Baker Street to help Mrs. Hudson with the travails of managing her rooms. He carried messages, cleaned living areas, prepared hearths, set tables, brushed clothing.

Conversing with a consulting detective served as a magnet for Billy as well. By the end of the first few weeks, in fact, he had developed a rapport with the very man who had found him out but a short time before. On any number of subjects from the criminal mind to Sarasate's violin concertos, they always seemed to find something to talk about. Nor should Holmes' interest in the lad be considered unusual.

Although my old friend had precious few encounters with children, his relationship with the Baker Street Irregulars, the street urchins who canvassed London at his beck and call, is legendary. The Irregulars could ingratiate themselves in all manner of ways an adult investigator could not. As effective as the boys were in blending into the background, so were they equally difficult to be remembered as individuals, the characteristic that helped make them so invisible and, therefore, successful. But Holmes worried about them constantly. So concerned was he over the welfare of his young *protégés* that one need not be surprised when later, as certain events came to threaten Billy, Holmes asked me, "How far am I justified in allowing him to be in danger?"

Thanks in great part to the notoriety of my accounts of Holmes' exploits that appeared regularly in magazines like *The Strand*, whenever I did get to Baker Street that spring, Billy would talk to me about writing. Studying the classics at school, he frequently interrogated me concerning literature. In particular, he asked about my own literary techniques, especially those that dealt with plotting. Of course, in the case of recounting factual occurrences like Holmes' and my numerous adventures, plotting in the traditional sense is less challenging—one generally lays out the events chronologically—that is, as they actually occur. To the novice, it might appear that all the reporter has to do is take them down. Yet one's muse constantly beckons, and I have always trusted that my faithful readers could forgive me the dramatic flair or overzealous embellishment I might have inadvertently inserted in some of Holmes' investigations.

To his credit, Billy recognized—dare I say, "appreciated"—my literary efforts and admitted that, if the opportunity ever presented itself, he too would like to try his hand at written composition. *Why not give the lad a chance to sharpen his nib on an actual case?* I wondered. *What problems can that cause?* Little did I imagine that, when providence provided the opportunity in the tale that I titled "The Adventure of the Mazarin Stone", I myself would be the recipient of those slings and arrows that in all fairness should have been directed at the novice.

The events of the case in question were brief, simple, and straightforward. In the summer of 1903, just months after Billy's arrival at Baker Street, the Mazarin stone, a diamond worth at least a hundred thousand pounds, was stolen from Lord Cantlemere, and he called upon Holmes to find it. Thanks to the obtuseness of the thief, who in Holmes' very sitting room, confessed to his partner of having it upon his person, Holmes was able to snatch the jewel, return it to its rightful owner, and hand the culprits over to Inspector Youghal of Scotland Yard. If there were any clever trick involved in Holmes' approach, it was the playing of a violin recording in another room to fool the thieves into thinking that Holmes himself was actually bowing and therefore too preoccupied and far away to overhear their personal conversation. In fact,

Holmes was holding a glass to the closed door and listening to everything the miscreants had to say. It was a simple tale whose actions were confined to our sitting room. In short, the story seemed perfect for Billy to dramatize because it offered him little chance of going astray. Or so I thought.

To see what sort of narrative Billy might construct, I handed over to him the brief notes I had made from Holmes' report not long after the case's conclusion. Ironically, because the account the lad had composed has so often been mistakenly published as one of my own, the story's authorship has wrongly been attributed to me. My word! When a Holmes case begins with third-person references to me, John H. Watson, the customary first-person chronicler of my friend's exploits, only the most thick-headed of readers could possibly conclude that I was the story's true author. Moreover, with a string of flattering adjectives like "wise," "tactful," and "imperturbable" to describe the pageboy, one need not be Sherlock Holmes to identify the page himself as the rightful, if vainglorious, composer of the piece.

But I anticipate myself once more. Let me state that on my next visit to Baker Street following Billy's receipt of my notes, the boy eagerly handed me the account he had concocted. Although I was more concerned with Holmes' tired appearance than Billy's literary accomplishments, upon my return to Queen Anne Street I bade my wife goodnight, poured myself a glass of port, and settled into a wing chair to read the heralded manuscript.

Granted his youth, the lad wrote well, and his overly embellished version of Holmes' simple tale began accurately enough with Holmes' own report of the stolen diamond. But then poor Billy turned to flights of fancy. For example, to emphasize the importance of the valuable stone, Billy recorded an imaginary visit to Baker Street by the Prime Minister. To heighten the drama, he appropriated from my own account of "The Empty House" a wax figure representing Holmes, which in that earlier story my friend had placed in the bow window as a target for would-be assassins. True enough, the suspected thieves—Count Negretto Sylvius and his dim partner in crime, the boxer Sam Merton—did arrive at Baker Street with the intent to intimidate Holmes. So confident did they feel that, once the miscreants believed Holmes to be off in his room playing the violin, Sylvius removed the valuable stone from his pocket to show it off to Merton. At this point in reality, Holmes simply reappeared through the doorway and grabbed the diamond. But Billy's Holmes pounces on the thieves and retakes the stone only after switching places with Billy's newly re-invented wax effigy, an effigy which had been placed in the sitting room by means of a side-door that, like the wax figure itself, exists solely in the boy's imagination. At the end, as in reality, Inspector Youghal is summoned, and Holmes returns the diamond to Lord Cantlemere—but not before a preposterous *dénouement* in which a sardonic Holmes, trying to convince Lord Cantlemere that the jewel has been in Cantlemere's possession all along, surreptitiously slips the diamond into His Lordship's coat pocket.

Ω

Following my morning surgery the next week, I brought Billy's rolled-up manuscript to Baker Street. To keep it dry in the rain that was soaking the city that day, I transported it under the folds of my ulster. With one hand thus preoccupied, I needed the lad to help me remove my coat, but no sooner had he opened the door to let me into the entry hall than he began questioning me.

"Begging your pardon, sir," he said politely enough, "but might I ask what you thought of my story?"

"Give me a moment, won't you?" I replied, struggling to shed the wet coat while maintaining my hold on his precious manuscript. He did come to my aid, but I'm sure he was more interested in keeping his work dry than with my comfort. Together we climbed the stairs to Holmes' sitting room where Holmes, ever the sleuth, noticed the manuscript in my hand and deduced it was time for a convenient retreat. Leaving me to handle the novice writer, he rejected the fire in the hearth and retired to his bedroom.

Accompanied by a defiant Beethoven violin-sonata issuing from behind Holmes' closed door, I unrolled the pages of foolscap, squared them up on the cherry-wood table, took a deep breath and began. I pointed first to the start of the tale and then, riffling through the pages, I pointed to the finish. "Notice," I told the boy, "how a story reportedly about the skill and wisdom of Sherlock Holmes begins and ends with the appearance of Billy the page. While I do appreciate your full-circle intent, your ability to come back to where you started, if you feel that you yourself must play so prominent a role in the story, you might consider a first-person narrator—a fictional detective, for example, if crime writing becomes your *métier*."

"No offence, Doctor Watson," he said, "but I don't trust first-person narrators. They're never completely honest."

Rather than accepting the suggestion, I realized, he preferred the parry. "Better a forthright first-person narrator than a dissembling third," I countered.

Billy groaned, presumably understanding the lesson I was trying to teach. Criticising someone's writing is never easy, for the writer always hopes for the best. When the first critical strike hits, the result often evokes an inelegant but all-revealing sigh of deflation.

I persevered, nonetheless. "Look here," I said, pointing to another early paragraph. "Although you never mention them by name, see how you have boldly brought into the action Mr. Balfour—the Prime Minister himself—not to mention the Home Secretary, Mr. Akas-Douglas. Since I assume that Holmes would have informed me of any actual visit to Baker Street by such august personages, I can only infer that you have inserted them into your account as a way of giving it greater importance."

"Agreed," Billy said, "But sometimes reality needs help. You must know what I mean. Who could be fooled by that set-up of yours in 'The Red Headed League,' all those ginger-haired chaps engaged to trick just one?"

"It fooled Jabez Wilson," I replied, annoyed by his impertinence but inwardly pleased that he was so familiar with my stories. "After all, fooling Jabez Wilson was what happened in reality."

"Maybe so, but—"

"Your manuscript reads like a play," I said, cutting him off before he could digress from his own work even further. "To be sure, the action did occur in only one location—here—but you could have opened up the setting to include so much

39

more. The single scene is too claustrophobic. There's no exit and much-too-much dialogue unaccompanied by narrative description."

The crackling fire might easily have been heating up his ire as well as the room.

"But it bloody well *did* happen here!" he cried. "There's not much else to describe. It's all too simple; you yourself said to dress up the ruddy action."

Ignoring his crudities, I arched the fingers of my right hand on the foolscap. "Of course, you must engage your reader, my dear boy. But not at the expense of truth. Truth!" I waved my arms at the four walls around us as I spoke the holy word. "Truth! Where is the waiting room that you described in your story? And how did a door so magically appear beside the window alcove when in reality there is none?"

"I needed a way of getting Holmes and his effigy in and out of the bow," he proclaimed, holding his head high.

"But in actuality there was no effigy."

"There was in *your* bloody story, 'The Empty House.'"

I winced at his language, but he stood his ground. No apologies here, I noted as he ran his fingers through his sleek black hair.

"Yes, Billy," I said slowly, hoping to appease him. "There is indeed an effigy in that account. And I do appreciate your research—Dulwich is training you well. But there was an actual effigy in the true story. You cannot willy-nilly appropriate the material from one history and place it in another wherever you choose."

"What about your silly snake in "The Speckled Band"? No real snake can climb a bell rope."

"But it did, Billy. It really did. You must draw a distinction between what you merely imagine and what is real."

Suddenly, as if he was found out, Billy's shoulders sagged, and he lost his defiant pose. It was a reaction I'd seen many young writers exhibit at one point or another when confronted with realistic assessments of their so-called "art."

From somewhere deep inside, however, Billy found the courage to ask, "Is there nothing of merit in my work?"

"Of course, Billy." Fearing I might have been too harsh in my approach, I began anew. "I like your detail at the start— 'the scientific charts on the wall, the acid-charred bench of chemicals, the violin case leaning in the corner . . . the baggy parasol.' You're good at noting the fine points; offer your readers more. And I especially like your use of the vernacular—words like 'split' and 'peached.' The more such slang you attribute to the persons who use it, the more convincing your writing shall be. Your dialogue rings true. You have a wonderful ear for accurately reproducing how people speak—the criminal class in particular. Really, lad, you write very well. Just remember to be credible, honest, real and baffling all at the same time." I was overstating the case a trifle. "Relax," I cautioned, "and it will come. You have talent, lad. I can tell."

A faint smile began forming on Billy's lips. "My classics master, Mr. Hose, will be pleased," he said.

"But what I like most, young man," I said, pointing to two distinct passages in his manuscript, "is the insight you've displayed regarding our common friend, Mr. Holmes. In the three months you've been here, you rightly profess—as you yourself put it—to know his 'ways by now.' And thanks to that understanding, you perceptively write that Billy the page has 'helped a little to fill up the gaps of loneliness and isolation which surrounded Holmes.' Indeed, one can only hope that you are correct."

Obviously pleased with the complimentary aspects of the review, Billy took the papers from me and knocked on Holmes' door to inform him that the writing seminar had ended. "Maybe someday I'll compose a list of your rules," Billy said to me before marching downstairs to fetch our tea. 'Dr. Watson's Notes on Writing the Mystery Story' I could call it."

"Billy's a natural writer," I told Sherlock Holmes upon his return to the sitting room. "He has an extraordinary ability to record people's speech, a keen sense of detail, and excellent insight into human nature. I imagine that living with his mother has given him a greater sense of maturity than that of other schoolboys his age."

"And you called *me* a psychologist," Holmes said with a laugh.

Ignoring my friend's mocking tone, I persisted. "The lad needs practice. He needs more experience in writing; he needs more experience in life. Eventually, he must discover who he is and what he wants to write about. It's all up to Billy. He has to trust his natural abilities. One can only wonder where his compositional instincts will take him."

"Good old Watson," Holmes said, "a teacher till the end."

Despite the gloom outside, I enjoyed my tea that afternoon before the dancing fire.

III

The only salvation for a writer is to write.
--Raymond Chandler
The Long Goodbye

The next few months were bittersweet for Sherlock Holmes. Perhaps it was my fault, my inattentiveness—some might call it my abandonment of the man—which cost the world the services of so astute a consulting detective. Perhaps it was Holmes' desire for tranquillity. Whatever the precise cause, in the late summer of 1903, not long after the Mazarin Stone episode, he decided to give up his familiar rooms in Baker Street and retire. Regardless of how pleased his actions may have made the criminal elements, Holmes had been harbouring other plans for quite a while. As my readers have already come to learn, he moved to a small cottage in the South Downs where he hoped to realize his lifelong ambition: the maintenance, study, and documentation of a colony of bees with particular emphasis on the queen.

Holmes' departure from London affected many of us. I, for one, found myself spending more time at home with my wife while Mrs. Hudson, who ultimately would become Holmes' housekeeper in Sussex, had to seek new boarders at 221. Young Billy, upon discovering that his current school work required more attention than the previous year's curriculum, realized that he could return to full-time studies at Dulwich with a clear conscience and a new sense of self-confidence.

I would like to believe that Billy's writing experiences at Baker Street helped cultivate his commitment to the Classics. And yet, as I learned in an exchange of letters the following year, he had shifted—or, rather, had been forced to shift—his academic focus once more. Since his Uncle Ernest was footing the bill for the boy's education, Uncle Ernest could insist that Billy confine his attention to the Modern Side, the course of study that would prepare him for the world of business, rather than to the Classics, whose study—at least, according to Uncle Ernest—simply immersed its devotees in the impractical world of *belles-lettres.* Worse, Uncle Ernest was pressuring his nephew into leaving school entirely in order to learn the major mercantile languages of the Continent. Such knowledge would enable the lad to take up a trade, an accomplishment Uncle Ernest hoped Billy would achieve as soon as possible so his nephew could begin supporting not only himself but also Billy's mother.

Thus it came to pass in April of 1905 that the former page came round to Queen Anne Street to say good-bye. At the age of seventeen, he was abandoning Dulwich College and, with the blessings of his pragmatic uncle, going off to spend more than a year abroad, hoping to master the aspects of French and German that he would need in the commercial culture his uncle was forcing him to enter.

"I'll miss our discussions on writing," Billy said. His final words were, "Be sure to pass on my farewells to Mr. Holmes."

Although Billy and I had no communication for the next two years, he did finally send me a letter that described his European venture and ultimate return to England. He had begun his stay in Paris at the Pension Marjollet at 27 Boulevard St. Michel, which, to be *au courant*, he insisted on calling *'Boul' Mich'*. Not far from Notre Dame, his room was situated just above the Café Vachette, where Bohemians of all stripes would congregate. In a word, Billy's *pension* placed him at the centre of the swirling artistic movements of Paris in the period people have come to call *La Belle Époque*. Although a traditionalist like me might be put off by the iconoclastic attitudes of the modern French artists and authors of the time, I could at least recognize how a budding writer like Billy couldn't ask for better stimulation than what he must have encountered on the Left Bank in the first decade of the twentieth century.

In Paris, Billy had taken classes to learn French. When he travelled to Germany, he studied with a tutor, an approach he much preferred. For a while, he lived in Munich and then near the Black Forest in picturesque Freiburg im Breisgau, and he further cultivated his German-language skills on side trips to Nuremberg and Vienna.

But inevitably the time for travel had to an end. In the spring of 1907, Billy, now almost twenty, returned to England, which he seemed finally ready to accept as his home. Apparently, the British side of his nature had triumphed. In May, the American-born lad passed the required interview with a detective from Scotland Yard, took the oath of allegiance to the Crown and became a naturalized British citizen. By June, having earned high marks during the six-days of civil service examinations he had sat for in English, foreign languages, and maths, he secured a position at the Admiralty. Boasting of his third-place finish in a field of six hundred, he seemed poised to start his life anew.

And yet not all had changed. Despite his official citizenship and his new occupation, he still found the way back to his ever-worrying mother. By this time, his grandmother, the so-called "tyrant," had died; and Mrs. Chandler was living alone at 35 Mount Nod Road in Streatham some five miles south of central London. Billy decided to join his mother in her small, common house in a street full of small, common houses.

Even so, the winds of discontent were churning. Knowing Billy as Holmes and I did, we could have predicted that it wouldn't take him long to grow restless. But just how restless was another question. After only a few months at the Admiralty, he was already regarding the daily train ride to Whitehall and the tedious and dreary routine of his work as intolerable. For half a year he held a job, which, despite his great success in his examinations, he regarded as a glorified clerkship. As Assistant Stores Officer in the Naval Stores Branch, he was charged with keeping account of the movement of naval supplies. Overseeing the relocation of military necessities like ammunition might seem exciting to some, but Billy hated his work. Worse, he hated having to tip his hat to so-called superiors and being ordered about by people he called "suburban nobodies." He had his own life to live, his own career to shape; and neither included the British navy. Having inherited his mother's defiant nature, he quit his position and moved on.

Strangely, Uncle Ernest seemed to accept Billy's decision. Perhaps it was being coerced by his tyrannical mother into the role of solicitor that enabled Ernest to sympathize with his nephew. Whatever the reason, upon learning that Billy had severed ties with the Admiralty, Uncle Ernest remained true to his own practical nature. He recognized that with Billy out of work, he himself would need additional income, especially since he so enjoyed being a man of property. "A house in Forest Hill is a better investment than one in Streatham," is how Billy says his uncle reacted to Billy's news. Thus, Mrs. Chandler found herself in new digs, this time in a semi-detached house at 148 Devonshire Road in Forest Hill where Billy often joined her. The neighbourhood itself had a more village-like atmosphere than did working-class Streatham.

Perhaps young Billy had been a Bohemian from the start; perhaps his stay among the literati in Paris had struck a spark, or maybe the Siren song of writing was simply too great to withstand. Whatever the catalyst, Billy wound up finding himself a cheap room in a boarding house in Russell Square not far from the British Museum, the area of London called Bloomsbury that was only just then beginning to claim for itself the title of literary centre of the Empire.

At the same time, he wanted to share the news of his recent success. Hence, the letter he posted to me that, in addition to recounting his travels on the Continent and return to England, announced that he had secured a position as journalist with the *Daily Express*. It was thanks to my encouragement, Billy said, that he had hoped to become a writer, and here was the start. He even confessed to writing poetry. Admittedly composed in the bathroom, his first poem, entitled "The Unknown Love," was published by *Chambers's Journal* on 19 December 1908. To hear Billy tell it, most critics dismissed the piece. But in the long run, such criticism didn't matter. Thanks to the appearance of the poem—along with his job at the *Express*—Billy's literary career had officially begun.

Ω

Besides that last letter to me, as well as whatever of his publications I encountered in print, I heard nothing more of Billy the page until late one cold night in October of 1910. An intermittent rain had been washing the city. My wife and Mrs. Meeks, our housekeeper, had gone to bed, and I was reading the latest edition of a medical journal before a comforting fire when a loud rapping at our front door caused me to start. At first, I thought it was thunder, but the echoing rattle of the brass knocker convinced me that someone was actually pounding on the wooden door itself.

"Who's there?" I demanded before drawing the bolt aside.

"Billy," came the answer. "The page-boy from Baker Street, Dr. Watson."

"Billy?" I questioned. I hadn't laid eyes on him since he had left for the Continent some five years before. What could possibly bring him to my home so late at night?

Immediately, I threw open the door. Standing before me in what was now but a soft drizzle stood two men. Billy, with his wet black hair framing his face and his features leaner and older than I remembered, was literally holding up his slumping companion. Quite a picture they made, Billy in a buttoned dark mac; the other man, the one who needed the help to stand, sporting a red-plaid wool scarf and open black ulster over formal attire. But even more striking than the stranger's shaky constitution was its vividness. He appeared a young man, yet his matted wet hair was snow white, and scars corrugated the left side of his face from just below his eye down to his chin. Whether his left eye remained partially closed due to the scarring or to his attenuated condition, it was difficult to tell. Standing in the rain as they were, the latter draped on Billy who was struggling to keep him upright, they presented a most dramatic tableau.

"Come in, come in," I said, taking their coats and directing them into the sitting room with the fire crackling in the hearth.

"I'll get some brandy," I volunteered, but Billy shook me off.

"This is Terrence Leonard," he said. "I just met him tonight, and I'm afraid he's already had too much to drink. I found him lying in the street and didn't know for certain what was wrong with him. I knew you lived nearby. So I took the liberty of bringing him here."

A check of the stranger's eyes and a whiff of his breath confirmed Billy's diagnosis.

"You're right," I told Billy. "He's simply drunk too much alcohol,"

"I thought that was the case, but one never knows. That's why I wanted you to have a look at him, Doctor."

"The women of the house are asleep," I said. "I'll make coffee. With plenty of sugar."

I left to prepare the brew while Billy was arranging Terrence Leonard before the fire. Upon my return, Leonard's white head was still drooping, but he would occasionally jerk it upright in an effort to stay alert.

Billy and I managed to get him to the dining room table, and soon we were all savouring the hot coffee and sampling the scones and jam I was able to find in the larder.

"How did you meet your inebriated friend?" I asked Billy.

"I was writing a story this evening for the *Express*," he said. "At the Langham Hotel. Quite trivial, really—a social event—Lord Steynwood, the publisher, was celebrating his sixty-fifth birthday. My job was to note the important people who were there, describe what they were wearing, report any gossip I could overhear. I did my best though I'm not really interested in that sort of thing."

I knew the type of piece he was referring to. Silly goings-on. And yet I must say that accounts of such events provided exactly the kind of seemingly insignificant information from which Holmes could often glean the most valuable facts.

"As I was leaving," Billy continued, "a large motor-car—a Rolls Royce *Silver Ghost*, actually—arrived to pick up two passengers, this gentleman here and his beautiful red-headed companion."

Terrence Leonard opened his eyes. "My wife," he intoned, then shut them again.

"With the chauffeur's help, she entered the car, but Mr. Leonard stumbled as he climbed in, and the chauffeur couldn't close the door because Mr. Leonard's leg was hanging out.

When the chauffeur opened the door wider, Mr. Leonard slipped off the seat cushion and fell to the pavement. Above the raised voices of nearby drivers and pedestrians, I clearly heard the woman, his wife, shout, 'Take a cab!' Mrs. Leonard ordered the driver back into the car, and immediately thereafter, the Rolls drove off, leaving Mr. Leonard lying in the wet gutter."

The poor man in question held up his cup, and I poured him more coffee.

"It was quite a scene, really," Billy continued. "The rain had stopped, and the city was quite dark; but the empty roads were drenched enough to create reflecting images. Envision a black canvas full of shimmering lights and iridescent colours with Mr. Leonard here sprawled in the foreground." Billy pondered this juxtaposition for a moment, then added, "Even the most beautiful of landscapes can in an instant devolve into the meanest of scenes."

"My, my," I observed. "A philosopher as well as a poet."

"I had drunk too much, y' see," Leonard offered by way of explanation. He slurred many of his words and stammered as he spoke. "S-Sylvia—my wife—she wanted no more of me—I-I reckon I misspoke once too often at our dinner party— in the automobile I was drunk enough to have her throw me out."

"Which is where I found him," Billy said. "He was in such a state that he couldn't remember his address. That's when I recalled you lived close by, Doctor. I couldn't find a cab, but we managed the walk despite the rain."

I gazed at Terrence Leonard. Seemingly full of chagrin, he brushed away a tangle of wet hair from his forehead, a tangle of wet hair that was white as bone. "My recommendation," I said brusquely, "is the usual: avoid any more spirits and get plenty of rest."

"I'll take you to my mother's home in Forest Hill," Billy offered. "You can sleep it off in the drawing room, and I'll explain your presence to her in the morning."

It was settled; and Terrence Leonard, still unsteady on his feet, managed to thank me for my hospitality and, with the help of Billy, his newly-found friend, limped out.

As I closed the door on the two of them, I found myself hoping to see "charming Billy" again; of the peculiar Mr. Leonard, I had no reason to expect to hear anything more. I suppose that with the proper crystal ball, a spiritualist would not have surprised me by predicting that Billy might well reappear in my future; on the second point—the re-emergence of Terrence Leonard into my life—had the same spiritualist made that charge, I would have been very shocked indeed.

Ω

As I have documented elsewhere, by the start of 1911 Sherlock Holmes had been communing with his bees in Sussex for more than seven years. Mrs. Hudson had long-since agreed to take on the role of housekeeper at the cottage, and all the while Holmes did his very best to remain outside the riotous world of London. He might occasionally come up to attend a concert at the Royal Albert Hall or to study some arcane manuscript at the British Museum, and for those special events he and I would usually arrange a repast at some familiar restaurant like Simpson's.

As the mood struck, I myself might make the infrequent journey to the South Downs to see my old friend, but generally speaking my social activities greatly diminished following Holmes' departure from London. For me, most days consisted of maintaining my medical practice and performing the husbandly duties required to help run a household already stocked with wife and small staff. In short, life had become satisfyingly routine.

In late January, therefore, I was surprised to receive a dinner invitation from Billy. After all, I hadn't seen him since he'd arrived at my doorstep with his inebriated friend the previous October. While I must confess to wondering every now and again what fate had befallen the unfortunate Terrence Leonard, I do most readily admit to caring far more about how young Billy was faring. During that strange night a few months before, I had had little opportunity to find out the direction his writing career was taking. With all due humility, I thought that at the very least I might be able to offer some helpful suggestions regarding his work.

We had agreed to dine later that evening at an Italian restaurant he'd suggested in Southampton Row not far from his digs in Bloomsbury. It was another chilly winter's night in London, and darkness had fallen early. Keeping to one's own turf—as I had become so used to—makes it easy to forget how difficult getting about in the blowing wind and biting cold can be. Billy had wanted to *rendezvous* at a street corner rather than in his Bohemian den. But even with my thick tartan muffler, kid-leather gloves, and heavy overcoat, I did not fancy having to stand idly by stamping my feet until he arrived. Happily, I discerned him soon enough in the light of an electric street lamp near our appointed place of meeting. He raised a silver-headed walking stick as a form of hello.

"A gift to myself when I returned from the Continent," he said self-consciously of the stick as we shook gloved hands.

Although his face seemed thinner, he looked well; and after expressing the usual pleasantries, I followed his lead as we walked briskly along Southampton Row accompanied by the tap of his stick.

"It's just up the road," he said of the restaurant. I could see the vapour of his breath in the chilled night air.

Difficult as it was to conduct a conversation in the cold night air, I asked him how his literary career was progressing.

"Unless one is very good at it," he observed, "I'm afraid that earning a living from writing is a difficult prospect."

I nodded in agreement. *How would my own stories fare*, I wondered, *without the exploits of a hero like Sherlock Holmes to propel the action?*

"Sometimes," Billy said, "I think all my work is inferior. I'm very good at writing second-rate material, but warmed-over tripe is not what one's employers are seeking."

I was familiar with Billy's cynical nature; but despite the cold, this last comment brought me to a halt. I turned to look him in the eye.

"The *Express* dismissed me," he confessed, averting my glance. "I wasn't very good."

"Surely your writing is good enough for—"

"Dr. Watson," he interjected, "I got lost in the streets on my way to a story. I can't really complain."

I stamped my feet in an angry effort to keep warm.

"But not to worry," he said. "All is not darkness and gloom. I've returned to Dulwich."

A young adult returning to public school? I looked mystified.

"No, Dr. Watson, I'm not going to be a student again. *The Alleynian*, the college magazine, is going to publish some of my work. More importantly, at the start of this past Michaelmas term, Mr. Hose, my former Classics master, got me the position of substitute teacher. I'm being paid only about fifty-three pounds, but at least it's steady work."

The good news enabled me to breathe more easily. Holding on to the positive made me realize just how much I'd been wishing for his success from the very start—from our very first discussion about his version of 'The Mazarin Stone'. After his initial resistance, Billy had opened up to suggestions. He'd become willing to learn—characteristics bound to help him in the future. Perhaps, he would succeed on his own after all. *Listen to me,* I thought, *feeling every bit like a proud father.*

But I was also feeling quite cold. Placing my arm around his shoulder, I indicated we should resume our walking; and though I immediately retracted my arm, we continued marching up the road in unison.

"Here's something more you'll enjoy," he went on. "As much as I don't like accepting favours, my Uncle Ernest knows someone who knows a gentleman with connections at *The Westminster Gazette*. They've already accepted a few of my poems. And *The Academy* has agreed to print some of my work as well."

Obviously, my worrying had begun too soon. The lad seemed to be looking after himself quite well. It would appear that the essays and book reviews (albeit of mainly minor works) that constituted Billy's serious literary production would, despite his misfortune at the *Daily Express*, still provide him the opportunity to be published.

"What about your poetry?" I asked. "What sort of poems have you been writing?"

"Oh," he exclaimed with even more enthusiasm, "I write all types. After all—" and here he began proudly to recite—"'Beside the grimmest tragedy/A witness I must stand, /Long buried griefs are near to me /As my ink-spattered hand.'"

My quizzical looked elicited an explanation: "From a poem I call 'The Poet's Knowledge.' But to answer your question about what sort of poems I prefer, I suppose—like many others poets nowadays—I find myself drawn to medieval romance. I've already published a number of poems along those lines in *The Gazette*. I wrote one called 'The Quest' and another called 'When I Was King.' Then there's 'The Perfect Knight' and 'A Pilgrim in Meditation.' Last year, *The Spectator* published 'The Death of the King.'"

"And what draws you to those medieval days of yore?"

"That's a good question, Dr. Watson. Sometimes I think I owe it all to a medieval-style painting by G.F. Watts called *Galahad*. There's a large photograph of it in the library back at Dulwich. I used to look at it every day: Galahad standing next to his white horse. I often think I'd like to be a knight like Galahad—wearing shining armour and looking pensive and relaxed. And yet at the same time he appears ready to ride off and save some lady, probably naked, who might be in distress. Gathering up naked women was the kind of things those fellows did back then—Galahad; his father, Lancelot. Life seemed so much simpler in those days."

"Agreed," I said, although it must be noted that, even in Billy's simpler world, collecting other people's women could cause problems.

The cold did not allow me to ponder his imagery for long. I was, in fact, about to ask how much farther our destination was when we came upon a small group of people who, despite the chill, were crowding round the front of a shuttered bookshop. Although Billy and I stood behind the outer ring, I could easily see that they were all looking at something—someone, actually. Seated on the icy pavement, a man was propped up against the wall of the shop, groggily moving his head back and forth. And not just any man. For thanks to the white hair and scarred face, it took but a moment for both of us to realize that the poor creature was none other than Billy's friend, Terrence Leonard.

At first, I feared that he'd been accosted and, using my authority as a physician, I pushed my way through the throng. But as previously, Leonard revealed no injuries or maladies, no sudden sicknesses or attacks. What other term can I use? He was simply drunk—again.

In the shadows nearby loomed a public house, the Crown and Eagle, no doubt the source of Leonard's unfortunate spirits.

Anger grew in both Billy and me. After all, had not the helpless man before us pledged that he would reform?

Just then a gruff voice rose above the gawpers' murmurings. "Make way. Make way." A police constable wrapped in a dark heavy coat was using both elbows to force a path through the crowd. With shop lights reflecting off his helmet badge, he looked like a beacon in the night.

"What's all this then?" he trumpeted when he reached the decrepit figure that was still hunched on the ground.

"It's all right, officer," Billy intervened. "I know the man. He's not feeling well." And Billy, handing me his walking stick, bent down to help Leonard to his feet.

"Think I hain't never seen a sozzlehead afore?" the policeman snorted. "Get 'im out of 'ere—that's all I ask. Save me the trouble of running 'im in, won't it?"

By now Leonard was up, an arm draped round Billy's shoulder. It was as if the two men had intentionally posed to recreate the identical tableau that had greeted me when I'd opened the door to them the previous October. Like the receding tide, the crowd drew back as the pair moved forward—as if not to be tainted by touching the odious derelict.

"Dr. Watson," Billy said, " I'm sorry about dinner, but I must take him home." And while I saw only futility in trying to help the unfortunate soul teetering before me, I nonetheless admired the pluck of young Billy for offering him aid.

"I'll hail a cab," I said, raising an arm and looking down the road.

Almost immediately, a hansom arrived, and I helped Billy get Leonard inside. This time I hoped the poor wretch could remember where he lived.

Once they were gone, I found myself standing alone at the kerb. The curious onlookers, having nothing more to see, had meandered off to their more customary haunts. Much to my surprise, I discovered that I was still holding Billy's silver-headed walking stick.

No longer with a partner for dinner, I reckoned that I might as well put the stick to good use and waved it at a passing cab. I could only wish that when I returned home, I would find a piece of cold roast beef waiting for me in the larder.

Ω

Just as I'd received no immediate news from Billy following the first unhappy incident involving Mr. Leonard, I received no word from him following the second. Not even my note to the lad regarding his forgotten walking stick elicited a response. What I suspected was that, having noted my earlier condemnation of his acquaintance, Billy was simply trying to avoid more of the same.

Happily, I was not ignored forever. Some six months later—on Tuesday, 11 July, to be precise—I received a brief letter from Billy inviting me for refreshment the following afternoon. I was to meet him at the Crown and Eagle, the sinister-looking public house in Bloomsbury next to which we had encountered the fallen Terrence Leonard.

Unlike my previous sojourn in Southampton Row, Wednesday's bright sun provided plenty of warmth for an invigorating walk; and Billy's stick, which I planned to return to him, aided my steps. Motor-cars and hansoms occupied the roadway, and people strode purposely to and fro among the many shops and stalls and office blocks. Even the public house, so dark and ominous when I first espied it, offered an oasis of welcome tranquillity within the bustling neighbourhood. One could well understand why Billy enjoyed spending time in the taproom amidst the dark hardwood panels, shiny brass fittings, and porcelain draw-handles.

Billy arrived a few minutes after I did. By that time, I'd already found a small table and begun rejuvenating myself with a pint of Guinness; he ordered the same. Although I noted with some concern that he and the publican seemed old friends, Billy and I greeted each other warmly; and with great fanfare I returned to him his silver-headed cane. It seemed just the thing to complement the boater with its school-tie band that he was currently sporting.

We exchanged the usual pleasantries; and then with slight trepidation based on past experience, I dared to ask Billy about his work.

"I just completed my teaching post at the College," he reported. "It went very well."

"Good," I replied with relief. "And your writing?"

"My writing," he repeated with little enthusiasm. "Oh, I'm still contributing poems to *The Gazette* and *The Academy,* and *The Alleynian* has taken some of my other pieces." Granted that his successes were limited, but even those few should have produced some joy. Yet he spoke with no excitement. Indeed, much to my amazement, he announced, "What I really wanted to talk to you about is how my friend Terrence Leonard is managing."

"Your *friend?*" I could not prevent a judgemental scowl.

"Things are different now," Billy said. "It's been months since he made that beastly appearance at your house the first time you saw him."

"And the second," I put in.

"Agreed. But I wanted to meet today so I could tell you how he's got himself back on a solid footing. I thought you should know—to set the record straight. A rich friend offered him a job for a few months that got him settled."

Imagining the scarred face of Terrence Leonard frightening away the customers in any sort of reputable establishment, I asked sceptically, "A job doing what?"

"I believe he acted as some sort of steward in a gentlemen's club, someone who helped maintain the order and such."

"A gentlemen's club," I scoffed. "Do you know what it's called?"

"The Tankerville. Near St. James's Square."

"The Tankerville," I repeated, vaguely recognizing the name. "Some sort of playing-cards scandal associated with the place a number of years ago. If I remember correctly, Sherlock Holmes helped clear a British officer accused of cheating at the card table."

"Dr. Watson, you yourself just said that's ancient history. I'm sure the club's reputation has improved."

"No," I said, trying to recreate the story in my mind, "there was something else—"

"Whatever it was," Billy interrupted, "working there helped Terrence re-establish himself. In fact, he's resumed living with his wife. They make their home in Marlow, not thirty miles from here—although he does comes into the city every so often to the family's town house in Mayfair."

"Mayfair," I observed. "So that's where he lives. Funny how he couldn't remember. With a house in that district and another in Marlow, I shouldn't doubt there must be quite a bit of money in his family."

"His wife Sylvia's family, actually," Billy said. "Her father is Lord Steynwood."

"Lord Steynwood? The publisher?"

Billy nodded.

"Just a moment," I said. "Weren't you writing a piece about Lord Steynwood's birthday celebration that night you first met Terrence Leonard?"

Billy laughed. "You can see how poor a reporter I was. At the time, I didn't even realize that Terrence's wife is Lord Steynwood's daughter."

"Why, Lord Steynwood is worth millions!"

"I know all that. It was the family connection that Terrence told me about—how, following the death of Lord Steynwood's wife some twenty years ago, His Lordship raised Sylvia and her younger sister Cora on the family estate in Buckinghamshire—just outside Marlow."

"Lord Steynwood," I said again, still intrigued by the reference. "One of the most influential newspaper publishers in the country, and not always influential in the best of ways."

Billy shrugged. "Terrence and I don't comment on His Lordship's business. We just enjoy the odd drink together. We discovered the Crown and Eagle one evening when Terrence came round to my place. It's quiet. We like it, and we've spent many an evening here."

I held up my tankard. "A pint or two of stout every so often is no sin," I offered, "and yet . . . ." My voice trailed off as again I recalled the two occasions I had met the inebriated Mr. Leonard—once drunk in my home and the other, drunk on a public pavement not too far from where we were now sitting. Terrence Leonard, the son-in-law of one of the most powerful men in England. It was hard to digest.

"Actually," Billy said, "Terrence is a gin drinker. He's introduced me to cocktails made of gin and lime juice, Rose's Lime Juice. 'Gimlets' they're called."

Billy took a long drink and let out a contented sigh.

"Be careful, young man," I said, shaking my head. "Too much steady drinking at an early age can lead to a lifetime of toxic consumption."

Billy smiled as he took another pull on his Guinness. "Don't dwell so much on the drinking, Dr. Watson. Terrence and I idle away most of our time just talking. I've told him of my schooling and time on the Continent, and he's told me his own history."

"His own history," I scoffed, "some sordid tale, I should imagine."

"On the contrary, Doctor. He fought bravely in the Boer War."

"Do tell," I said, sceptically. "I'm the first to admire a noble war story."

"Terrence was in the Loyal North Lancashire Regiment under Colonel Robert Kekewich. As Terrence recounts it, some time in April 1902, they were camped at a hillside in a place called Rooiwal. The Boers had scouted it before our lot had dug in; seems like the Brits got sent there due to some cock-up elsewhere on the battlefield—two units assigned to the same spot or some such miscalculation."

"All too common, sad to say."

"When those *bittereinders* discovered our boys in a position the Boers had originally thought was clear, they charged us anyway. A brave show on their part, outnumbered as they were. They rode in on horseback, firing rifles as they came. They did overwhelm some of our mounted infantry, but ultimately our artillery put the blighters on the run."

I remembered something of the sort in the record of the war written by Dr. Doyle, my literary agent. His historical account was, in fact, the work that earned him his knighthood. Yet despite the story of Kekewich's men, Billy had told me nothing specific about Terrence Leonard.

"And your friend?" I asked. "What happened to him at Rooiwal?"

"As you know, Doctor, the Boers were masters at *guerrilla* fighting, however unsporting we might think such tactics to be."

"Quite," I agreed, recalling with anguish the horrific casualties I myself had witnessed in the service of Her Majesty in Afghanistan.

"They used hand bombs," Billy said, "sticks of dynamite they lit while on horseback and tossed into enemy positions."

"My God," I whispered.

"Terrence was positioned in front of a group of men when one of those sticks flew in. The others scattered as best they could, but Terrence had the presence of mind—or foolishness, depending on one's point of view—to dive for the awful thing, pick it up, and hurl it back—burning fuse and all. Unfortunately, the dynamite still detonated much too close to him. You've seen the results. He's a true hero."

I admit to softening my feelings against Leonard. Having been wounded myself, I know how the terrors of war can drive many a good man—many a war hero—to drink. Or worse.

"Terrence was invalided out of the army although, as you know, the war ended not long after that incident. He met his future wife, Lord Steynwood's daughter, in hospital here in London where she and her sister had volunteered to help wounded soldiers. Despite Terrence's frightful condition, he and Sylvia spent many happy years together."

Billy's picture of marital bliss did not resemble his earlier description of the troubled couple. "I remember the story you told about the two of them at the Langham," I reminded him, "how his wife drove off leaving him on the pavement. How well do they get along now? I dare say that, following the incident with the car, such conjugal visits to London must have become far fewer."

"Well," Billy shrugged, "they did live apart for a few months following that night. But you're too old-fashioned, Dr. Watson." He added a derisive laugh. "A little drinking and bickering among friends is all the rage. We modernists try not to be as stifled as you Victorians. Terrence has a lot of good traits. He's friendly, dependable, someone you can talk to."

"And if I may ask, what is it that the two of you talk about?"

"There's a lot going on in my head these days, Dr. Watson. Women. Writing. My mum. Terrence has lots of good suggestions."

"I'm sure he does. Perhaps he should listen to his own advice first and fix up his marriage before he begins telling others how to behave."

Billy lifted his tankard for a final swallow. A small amount of stout pooled at the bottom, while remnants of white froth, like ladders of spider webs, clung to the sides. "Dr. Watson," he said, holding the glass before his lips, "Terrence and Sylvia have got back together. That's what I wanted to tell you. I'm certain things between them are going to improve. They always do." Following this pronouncement, he finished what was left of the drink.

The thump of the tankard as he returned it to the table punctuated his final sentence with the certainty of an exclamation mark.

IV

When in doubt have a man come through the door with a gun in his hand.
--Raymond Chandler
Introduction
Trouble Is My Business

A narrow path of light-brown cobblestones leads round the side of my Queen Anne Street house to the entry of my surgery. Inside the patients' waiting room facing the japanned door sits my nurse, Miss Shelvington, a middle-aged, thickset woman clad in white. Before her is the receiving table where she daily records the names and complaints of my patients as they enter and then offers them seats in one of the available bow-back chairs. Having got them settled, she lays the latest medical report underneath the others in the flat wooden box that sits on the small table next to the door of my consulting room. As I complete my work with each patient, I survey the new top sheet in the flat box and summon the person so described. When called upon, Miss Shelvington helps me with whatever medical procedures are required. It is a system that has proved quite efficient over the years, and it was in operation on the dreary Wednesday morning one week after my pub visit with Billy.

Thanks to the lowering clouds that concealed the sun, one would have been hard-pressed to recognize the season as summer—and yet, rain or shine, duty called, and I was preparing to pick up the day's first medical report. Before I had the chance to exit my office, however, I heard a great commotion in the adjoining room; it seemed to issue from somewhere near the front door.

"Stop!" I distinctly heard Miss Shelvington shout. "You can't go in there!"

As I rushed into the waiting room to see what was the matter, I did manage to catch a glimpse of my next patient, the elderly Mrs. Wallingham, who suffered from migraines; but it was the activity going on at the reception table that demanded my attention. Attempting to wrench his left arm free from my nurse's iron grasp was the startling spectre of scar-faced, white-haired Terrence Leonard. Only when they both saw me approaching was Leonard able to break away.

"Miss Shelv—" I began, but was stopped cold in my tracks when I observed the small pistol in Leonard's right hand. For the moment, with the gun pointed downward, his arm hung limply at his side.

"Dr. Watson," she cried, "I tried to tell him you were engaged, but he burst right past me!" Miss Shelvington had not yet spied the weapon,

"I must speak with you now, Doctor," Leonard demanded. His eyes were bloodshot. "I know you're busy, but you must hear me out."

"The gun," I said. "Give it to me."

Miss Shelvington took the opportunity to scream; looking up, Mrs. Wallingham moved not a muscle, save to shape her lips in the form of a circle. At the same time, Terrence handed me the small pistol. It was a Derringer; and while I'm no expert in firearms, I knew enough to smell it and determine that it had not been recently fired. I removed its single bullet and put it and the gun into the pocket of my white coat.

"Now," I countered, "you've given quite a fright to my nurse and to my patient!"

"Damn your nurse!" he shouted with a wild gleam in his eyes. "Damn your confounded patient!" And then he had the effrontery to march into my consulting room.

For her part, Mrs. Wallingham, a most sympathetic soul, remained with her mouth agape. I seated my nurse beside her, spoke a few soothing words to them both, and told Miss Shelvington I had to attend to this emergency.

When I entered the consulting room, I saw Terrence Leonard with his back to me. He was leaning over my desk using both hands to support his upper frame. I closed the door behind me and was about to issue him a dire warning. But he spoke before I could utter a word.

"She's dead," he said. "Murdered."

""M-murdered? Wh-who?"

"Sylvia. My wife."

It took a moment for the shock to register. I'd never met her, of course, but Billy had told me stories. "You must inform the police," I said.

"No! What I must do is push off. They'll think *I* did it. I found her body in her father's town house. Then I left. With her gun. I went looking for Billy; he's been so decent to me, I thought he could help. But I couldn't find him, so I came here. Tell him what's happened. Tell him not to try looking for me.

69

I can only say that I haven't killed anyone. Now I must be gone."

Before I could raise the briefest of protests, he bolted from the surgery and disappeared somewhere out on Queen Anne Street. It was obvious that I couldn't stop him, but I certainly could try to find Billy. With an apology to Mrs. Wallingham and instructions to my nurse that I was out of the office for the remainder of the day, I sent a telegram to Billy's digs in Bloomsbury and another to his mother's house in Forest Hill. Certainly, at one of those two locations, I should be able to alert him to the emergency involving his friend Terrence Leonard.

Ω

It had already gone 8:00 that evening when Billy appeared at my door.

I had actually dispatched three telegrams earlier in the day, the two to Billy's addresses and the other to Inspector Youghal of Scotland Yard, who, in fact, had arrived but a few minutes before. Ignoring convention, Billy rushed into the sitting room well ahead of Mrs. Meeks, cutting off my description to the inspector of Terrence Leonard's frantic visit to my surgery earlier that day. The lad stopped short at his recognition of the detective. Perhaps a trifle more grey at the temples and a bit thicker round the middle, the moustachioed Youghal really hadn't changed much in appearance from that day years before when Billy the page had summoned him in the matter of the Mazarin Stone.

"I've been out all day," he said, catching his breath. "I just got your message."

"I'm sorry, Dr. Watson," Mrs. Meeks explained, "but the young man just pushed by me and—"

""That's all right, Mrs. Meeks," I reassured her. "We're dealing with a matter of great urgency."

Mrs. Meeks stalked off, mumbling to herself something about "young people today."

Pulling on his moustache, Inspector Youghal stared at the young man who was still breathing quickly. "Not Billy the page from Baker Street," he said at last, "not the boy what helped me find Lord Cantlemere's diamond all those years past?"

"The same," Billy said, "but it was Mr. Ho—"

"Terrence Leonard was here this morning," I broke in. I knew the lad was going to defend Sherlock Holmes, but this was not the time for debate. I cut him off in mid-sentence and recounted for Billy what I had already told Youghal—how Terrence Leonard had barged into my surgery, how he had been carrying his wife's Derringer, and how he had told me about her death.

Billy said nothing. He just stared at me; then he turned to the policeman.

Youghal pulled at his moustache again. "'Tis a fact, Dr. Watson," he observed, "that we are indeed investigating the murder of a woman at the Mayfair town house of Lord Steynwood. His older daughter Sylvia—Mrs. Terrence Leonard—she was bludgeoned to death almost beyond recognition."

"Bludgeoned?" I said.

"Yes, why do you ask?"

"It's just that Leonard had the gun. I assumed she was shot."

"No, Doctor. She was not. Quite a messy scene, actually. In the south drawing room. Blood and brains everywhere. A bullet would have been much neater. Lord Steynwood was at his club when the tragedy occurred; and the butler, a bloke named Norris, saw Leonard running out the front door."

"He's certain it was Leonard?" Billy asked in disbelief. He had turned quite pale at the inspector's graphic description.

"Oh, he was certain all right. 'White hair and scars,' he said, "which, as I understand it, describes the man in question. Yes, the butler was quite sure."

Billy sank into a nearby armchair. "I can't believe it."

"But Leonard proclaimed his innocence," I put in. "And when I saw him, he wasn't covered in blood as he would have been if he'd bludgeoned her as you said. Is there no room for doubt?"

"If doubt there is to be, Doctor," said the inspector, "it is rapidly disappearing with every additional moment Mr. Leonard is absent."

"I know the man," Billy said. "We've spent time together. He's not capable of such an unspeakable act."

Inspector Youghal smiled. "I remember you as a boy when you was working for Mrs. Hudson. It was you what fetched me to put the cuffs on those jewel thieves. But you see, son, not all criminals are so easy to detect as that Count Negretto Sylvius. If they were, our job at the Yard would be that much easier."

Billy's eyes narrowed. "I'm no longer a boy, Inspector. Are you suggesting that I've been taken in by a cowardly murderer who beat his own wife to death?"

Ignoring the question, Youghal produced a small notepad and yellow pencil from his coat pocket. Nostalgic recollections gone, he was now all business. "For the record, sir," he said to Billy, "may I ask where you were just past midnight?"

"In my digs in Bloomsbury. I say, are you—"

"Can anyone confirm that?"

A flustered Billy paused to consider. "I was writing all day. Listened through the walls to my neighbour playing Bach on his violin; but, no, the fellow never saw me. I bought some ham and cheese for early supper, returned to my room with it, ate, did some more writing, and went to bed. By myself."

"More's the pity," the inspector said. "Witnesses can be helpful. It's so much easier when we can eliminate suspects."

A look of alarm crossed Billy's face. He opened his mouth as if to speak, seemed to think better of it, and remained silent.

"Right then," Youghal said. "I'll be getting back to the Yard. We've already posted men at train stations and dockyards, but I fear the fugitive has got too early a lead on us."

He returned his notebook and pencil to his pocket. Then he picked up his derby from the entry-hall table and, placing the hat on his head, touched its brim with two fingers, and followed Mrs. Meeks to the door. About to make his exit, he suddenly stopped and turned.

"Doctor," he said to me, "I almost forgot. Terrence Leonard's Derringer. I'll be needing to take it back to the Yard."

"His *wife's* Derringer," Billy corrected.

It was strange that I had forgotten about the gun. Reaching into the pocket of the coat to which I'd transferred it, I produced the small weapon and placed it into the policeman's outstretched hand.

"His *wife's* gun," I repeated.

"And who was it, Doctor, that told you this gun belonged to his wife?—besides Billy here, of course. The killer himself?" With a smirk and a shake of the head, Youghal examined the Derringer. "It's not loaded."

"Nor has it been fired recently," I told him. "I checked."

Youghal nodded his thanks and once more extended his hand. "The bullet as well."

"I thought it safer to remove it," I said, handing him the tiny missile that I'd kept in a pocket of my waistcoat."

Youghal grunted thanks. Then he resumed his original march out into the darkness.

Ω

Much against my better judgement, I had agreed to meet Billy in front of Lord Steynwood's town house shortly after noon the next day in Mayfair. Confident in his friend's innocence, Billy hoped that the key to the "true" story of Sylvia Leonard's murder might lie with the house staff.

No matter how determined Billy might be, I still had a medical practice to attend. As far as I was concerned, the terrible events of the day before needed to be put behind us, and the best method for accomplishing such a task seemed to me a return to routine activities as soon as possible. Still, I couldn't ignore Billy's pleas. After mollifying Miss Shelvington, as well as devoting additional examination time to Mrs. Wallingham and three others, I found myself in Mayfair beneath gloomy skies an hour or so after noon. I met Billy as we had planned. Dressed in his dark mac, he was leaning against the black wrought-iron fence that fronted the Steynwood property.

A stately terraced house that befitted its wealthy owner, it was painted like its neighbours' homes in a white the colour of rich cream. With windows trimmed in formal black and a pair of Corinthian columns framing the entrance, the stoic façade seemed unmoved by the tragedy inside. And yet one felt something ominous clinging to the place. A line of tall oaks near the pavement cast deep shadows across the large front door; and half-drawn curtains, like half-closed, calculating eyes, suggested an air of concealment. The centurion-like constable stationed at the front steps with his arms folded across his chest added to the sense of foreboding. So did the black police motor-car standing at the kerb.

Despite such gravity, Billy was sporting a wide grin.

"There's death within those walls," I said to him. "Why do you look like the cat that swallowed the canary?"

"Because," he said proudly, "I found out a lot from Ivy, the scullery maid. Thanks to my days in service with Mrs.

Hudson, I know how to be humble enough to approach the servant class."

I grunted at his false modesty.

He ignored my scepticism and went on about the maid. "She'd just finished washing the kitchen floor and was behind the house pouring out the dirty water. From her I learned that it was Nancy, the parlour maid, who'd heard from Mrs. Leonard's maid Violet, what had happened."

Ivy, Nancy, Violet. Billy seemed in his element when talking about women. "You simply smiled at her, and she brought out this Nancy to talk with you—is that it?"

Billy nodded, running a hand through his thick dark hair. "Yes, Dr. Watson, that's exactly what happened. Get past my crooked nose, and I'm a cute enough fellow. But even the scullery maid could tell that Nancy was in need of a man, and here was one on the doorstep, as it were, who wanted to speak with her—since Nancy was the one who'd conversed with Violet."

"A fact which you probably didn't emphasize in arranging your tryst."

"Right again. Nancy ambled out to the back, saw me and smoothed down her billowing black skirt. She twisted round her index finger a side-curl that had worked its way out from under her white cap."

Anticipating that Billy was about to produce some intimate details, I reasoned that neither the constable at the front door nor anyone else with more than a passing interest needed to overhear our conversation.

"Before you provide any lurid information," I said softly, "let's move down the road." I held out my arm to indicate the direction, and Billy and I innocently sauntered past a couple of neighbouring houses and stopped beneath the branches of one of the kerbside oaks. The shadow of its leaves added to the darkness of the afternoon.

"And so," I began again, "just what did you learn from the parlour maid?"

Billy took a deep breath and resumed his narrative: "Nancy told me that Violet McGee—"

"Mrs. Leonard's maid?"

Billy nodded, annoyed by my interruption. "Violet McGee," he began again with a dollop of sarcasm, "*Mrs. Leonard's maid,* entered the bedroom early yesterday morning with her mistress' breakfast. The room was empty. Violet couldn't find her mistress upstairs, so she proceeded to the ground floor. When she reached the smaller drawing room, she discovered its doors were locked and got Norris the butler to unlock them. When she entered, she discovered her mistress lying on the floor in her nightdress and Terence standing over her. There was blood all round, and we already know that Mrs. Leonard's head was terribly battered. Violet screamed for help. It was at this moment that Terrence pushed past Norris, who was still in the hallway, and ran up the stairs. Presumably, this was when Terrence must have picked up his wife's gun. Then he bolted. Lord Steynwood, who was summoned from his club, immediately called Dr. Goring, his daughter Cora's husband. Then Lord Steynwood called Scotland Yard. Needless to say, suspicion immediately fell on Terrence for having fled the scene."

"A very thorough report."

"Except that Sylvia Leonard's still dead," he said.

"From your account, there seemed to be no great weeping in the house. People going on about their daily business. No one too broken up by Mrs. Leonard's death, were they?"

"No, none of the servants seemed too distraught—that is, except Violet who discovered the body. I was actually going to ask more questions about Mrs. Leonard's relationships with the staff, but Norris himself came outside to retrieve poor Nancy. The scullery maid had obviously done some talking."

"And did Norris have anything of interest to say?"

"Only that the maids were to show me great distance as I was a friend of the man who had murdered their mistress."

"And His Lordship? Where is he?"

"Not out at the back where the scullery-maid empties her water, that's certain. In a word, I don't know."

"Given these further details," I said, "how do you now feel about your friend's guilt?"

Billy's eyes pierced the dappled shadows created by the leaves. "I know he's a strange character, Dr. Watson, but I don't think he's a killer. I can't imagine who committed this horrible deed, and I don't know how to find out. Still, I want to help as much as I can. If the true murderer ever *is* discovered, I'm sure Terrence will return from wherever he's run off to."

In the midst of telling him that I hoped he was correct, I detected movement up the road; in point of fact, the front door of the Steynwood house had opened, and Inspector Youghal, accompanied by two uniformed constables, was marching down the short staircase.

As they walked towards the police motor-car, Youghal spied the two of us huddling among the shadows. "Hullo," he cried, pointing at Billy, "the very man I'm looking for." He strode rapidly towards us, sweeping up the two constables in his wake.

"Billy the page," Youghal announced, eyes narrowing, " also known as Mr. Raymond Chandler?"

"Yes," Billy said.

"Inspector," I intervened, "you know who he is; you saw him last night at my home."

"Sir," he addressed Billy, maintaining his official tone as if I had not spoken, "we need you to accompany us to the station. I was about to go looking for you in Bloomsbury, but you have saved me the trouble. We found your name and address on a sheet of paper sitting atop Mr. Leonard's desk, and we have reason to believe that he was seeking your help following his brutal attack on his wife. Come along, please."

"Inspector," I said, my voice full of exasperation, "this is not new information. Leonard told me he went looking for Billy after he'd left the house. It was only when he couldn't find Billy that he came to my surgery."

Still paying me no mind, Youghal nodded at his men; and the two constables grabbed Billy's upper arms and escorted him to the awaiting car.

"Get Mr. Holmes!" Billy was able to shout before they unceremoniously shoved him into the vehicle.

"My thought exactly," I said to myself as the car was rumbling off down the road, belching clouds of black smoke.

I turned and walked rapidly—indeed, almost ran—to the nearest telegraph-office.

"*Come quickly*," I wired Holmes in Sussex, "*Billy is in trouble.*"

Ω

A hansom brought me to the Victoria Embankment where looms the Victorian-Gothic police headquarters commonly known as Scotland Yard. The massive structure is imposing enough to the innocent bystander; one can only imagine how ominous its red and white stonework and turrets must look to someone being taken inside for questioning. I didn't believe for a moment that, beyond Billy's friendship with Terrence Leonard, the lad had any connection to the murder of Lord Steynwood's daughter. But the risk of Billy's being manhandled by an overly zealous constabulary prompted my concern. At the very least, I wanted Youghal to know that Billy was being looked out for.

After making my way through a warren of indistinguishable hallways and offices, I found the Criminal Investigation Department. A beetle-browed sergeant sat at a desk near the doorway, and I told him that it was imperative that I saw the inspector.

"Not accepting visitors today, is he, Guv?" the sergeant replied calmly.

"Now see here," I responded angrily, "I must—"

"Try again tomorrow, yeh?" he said with a wink.

His relaxed demeanour irritated me all the more. "Tell him—"

"Inspector Youghal?" he added with a chuckle, "he might be receiving guests tomorrow at tea time."

It was obvious that I wasn't getting past this Keeper of the Gate. Exasperated, I marched out of the building.

Muted sunlight still washed the summer sky in shades of pastel pink, but the afternoon was turning into evening—too late, I thought, for a visit to my solicitor. Yet I couldn't forsake Billy. I returned to Scotland Yard twice that evening to send notes in to him, and I was troubled that my communications had gone unanswered. I could only assume that the police were detaining him over night to badger him into giving them the information they wanted to hear.

While Billy remained uppermost in my mind, I also had my surgery to consider. With patients scheduled for Friday morning, I tried reassuring myself that at least I knew where Billy was. In police custody, he couldn't get into any more trouble playing detective. On the other hand, I didn't want to leave him to the mercy of the police—not with Inspector Youghal's interrogation methods in mind. As soon as I'd seen my patients, I would return to Scotland Yard and renew my demands for his release.

Truth be told, although I hadn't yet heard from Holmes, I was still hoping that he might end up accompanying me. Not that I was worried that he hadn't responded to my wire. While Holmes could always be relied upon to furnish immediate aid, he wasn't the most punctilious of correspondents. Indeed, he regarded the contents of needless communications as useless facts. "It is of the highest importance, Watson," he told me long ago, "not to have useless facts elbowing out the useful ones."

Ω

"Mrs. Titmus," Miss Shelvington whispered to me Friday morning as I entered the surgery. She was referring to a new patient, the heavily made-up, elderly woman dressed in sombre black who was seated in my waiting room. Although no rain seemed imminent, Mrs. Titmus was accoutred with a baggy parasol, which just then was leaning against a neighbouring chair. I introduced myself; and picking up from the flat box near the doorway my nurse's report, invited Mrs. Titmus into my consulting room. After she'd grasped her parasol and got to her feet, I could see that, despite her mild stoop, she was quite tall and thin.

We settled opposite each other at my desk, and I quickly read over Miss Shelvington's notes.

"It would appear, Mrs. Titmus, that you suffer from a sore throat," I observed.

"Yes," she answered in what amounted to a stage whisper. "It hurts to swallow."

I thought I detected a Yorkshire inflection.

"Allow me to have a look, won't you?" I asked as, wooden tongue depressor in hand, I made my way round the desk.

She visibly stiffened when I approached her mouth, and from so close a distance I could easily see the thick rouge applied to her cheeks. I peered into the cavern of her afflicted throat, but could detect no signs of inflammation or infection. Indeed, I began to wonder whether she was some sort of hypochondriac who was wasting my time. The world is full of patients who seem to enjoy their occasions in a doctor's surgery; to them, it is like sitting for tea. While Billy remained in confinement, I had to humour this woman's whims. And then there was the whereabouts of Sherlock Holmes to occupy my thoughts.

"Frankly, Mrs. Titmus," I said, stepping back, "I find very little to comment on in your throat. Are you sure that is what truly bothers you?"

"Here," she responded in a hoarse voice, "What do you take me for—some sort of charlatan? I tell you that my throat has reduced me to whispers."

I felt most unprofessional to have so forcefully challenged a patient seeking help. "Let me consult a medical book, Madam. Perhaps I need to reconsider my diagnosis. Some oesophageal affliction may have escaped my memory."

I turned to the bookshelf behind my desk to survey a series of spines bound in green leather. I had just fingered the tome likely to contain what I was seeking when from behind me I was astounded to hear a familiar voice, "I can only hope, Watson, that you haven't erased *me* from your memory as easily as some 'oesophageal affliction'."

With a hearty laugh, Sherlock Holmes, swept the grey curls from atop his head and straightened to his true height. Although still made up in that garish face paint, he no longer resembled the old lady who had entered my office.

"H-Holmes," I gasped, forced to take a seat, "you—you never fail to surprise me."

"Not even with this?" he asked, raising before me the baggy parasol. "It is, after all, the old brolly from Baker Street—the same one I used to fool Negretto in recovering the stolen diamond."

I remained speechless, fooled once again by my old friend.

"You remember, Watson. 'The Mazarin Stone'? Billy described the brolly in that story he wrote all those years ago?"

"Billy!" I said. Immediately composing myself, I quickly reported to Holmes all that had transpired the day before—the murder of Sylvia Leonard, Terrence Leonard's appearance at my surgery, my meeting with Billy in front of Lord Steynbrook's home, and the young man's subsequent detention by the police.

"I assumed this *charade*, Watson, to prevent the eyes and ears of Lord Steynwood or anyone else from interfering with my journey to London. But now that I am here, I can dispose of this paraphernalia. We must go see Youghal as soon as possible."

I showed Holmes to his room where he could wash the make-up from his face and change his clothing. He had kept his more traditional attire in a Gladstone carefully hidden near the front door of my surgery.

The duplicitous Mrs. Titmus turned out to be my only patient that morning, the two others who were scheduled having failed to arrive. When my friend re-appeared as Sherlock Holmes, therefore, the two of us could immediately set off for Scotland Yard. On the way, I furnished Holmes the details that Billy had secured from Nancy the parlour maid relating to the murder of Sylvia Leonard. I also reported to him on the valiant service to her Majesty that Terrence Leonard had performed in South Africa. With the charges against Leonard so bleak, I thought some attempt should be made to balance the books. Although Holmes and I spent most of the trip to Scotland Yard discussing Terrence Leonard, it can't be said that our thoughts ever strayed too far from the well-being of Billy the page.

V

What did it matter where you lay once you were dead? . . . You were dead,
you were sleeping the big sleep, you were not bothered by things like that.
--Raymond Chandler
The Big Sleep

Clearly, the name of Sherlock Holmes opened more
doors at Scotland Yard than did mine. With the beetle-browed
sergeant from the day before nowhere to be seen, Youghal
himself brought Billy out to us at the long counter at the front
of the C.I.D office.

"Come all the way up from Sussex for your pageboy,
have you, Mr. Holmes?" Such was the detective's greeting to
my friend. "Well," he said, opening the little gate at the end of
the counter, "you can have him back." And Youghal gave
Billy a little shove in our direction. "We still think he knows
where Mr. Leonard got himself off to," the inspector said, "but
a night of questioning didn't get it out of him, so we'll cut him
loose for the time being." Dark half-circles beneath the
policeman's eyes suggested that he himself had been
personally involved in the so-called interrogation session.

It was with a grateful sigh that a haggard-looking Billy
stumbled over to Holmes and me on our side of the wooden
railing.

"If any harm has come to this lad—" I began.

But Holmes cut me off. "Now that I'm here in
London," he said to the Inspector, "I should very much like to

see the scene of Sylvia Leonard's murder. I expect that you can arrange admission for us to Lord Steynwood's town house."

Holmes' suggestion seemed to revive Billy. At the same time, a smirk worked its way into the policeman's tired face. "I won't say that I'd turn down your help, Mr. Holmes, but I don't believe that you'll be uncovering anything that my lads haven't already found. Terrence Leonard beat his wife to death, and there's the end to it. Still, I can't deny that you've been an aid in the past, and I don't see why you shouldn't give it a go."

"His Lordship won't object?" I asked, focusing on Holmes' plans instead of Billy's ordeal.

The inspector's tired face smiled more broadly this time. "Oh, Dr. Watson," he said, "I have no scruples when it comes to disturbing the leisure time of the idle rich."

Or the falsely accused, I thought. But rather than prolonging my outrage, I turned to Billy. "Are you feeling fit enough to make the trip?"

"Yes, sir," he replied, straightening up. "I'd love to try my hand at examining the murder scene."

With a sarcastic snigger, Youghal led us outside. We followed him across the road to the nearby police garage and stables where he requested a vehicle. We had to wait a few minutes, but eventually we heard the slow clip-clop of hooves. Moments later, a pair of matching coal-black horses pulling an enclosed black van came to a stop before us.

"Surely, not for us?" I said. No modern motor-car like the one Youghal had commandeered the previous day, the so-called "Black Maria" was a wagon usually reserved for the transporting of prisoners.

"We make do," Youghal shrugged, nodding at the driver. We followed the detective round to the back where he opened the rear door and climbed into the small, dank compartment. Holmes, Billy, and I followed. At least, the thick wooden door, through whose small barred window in its middle a few rays of light penetrated, thankfully remained unlocked. Accompanied by the plodding hooves of the horses, we clattered our way across the city to Mayfair.

Ω

Nothing had changed. Despite the shade from the trees in the front of the house, I could easily discern the burly constable with his arms behind him still standing at the front door. Once he espied Inspector Youghal climbing out of the van, he straightened his stance. The rest of us followed suit, extricating ourselves from the tight quarters, then stretching our legs and swinging our arms to get the circulation flowing again. The inspector marched up the front steps where Norris the butler spoke to him. Norris had opened the door only halfway but after a few hushed words with Youghal, pulled it wide and ushered us in. The butler led us through the entry hall and past the sweeping grand staircase, the cavernous north drawing-room, and the multi-volume library. He stopped before a small, salon with three sets of large French windows.

"The south drawing-room," Norris announced.

As soon as the butler left us, we four converged just inside the threshold. Sparsely furnished, the bright chamber might easily have been renamed the White Room. Its walls were papered in white floral patterns while white velvet curtains framed each of the three windows. A white jacquard settee and matching chair stood on one side of the room; a cherry-wood desk and chair, on the other. A light-blue oriental carpet with a flowery white border covered the floor, but it was the inharmonious claret-coloured stain at its centre that immediately caught the eye. The stain told us the obvious: that it was in this room that Sylvia Leonard had died. The family and staff had been ordered to stay out until Scotland Yard had completed the investigation; and Youghal insisted that, with the exception of the body, nothing had been moved or altered.

"At least, not intentionally," Holmes smirked. "With all those policeman traipsing about, who knows what damage has already been caused?"

Youghal ignored the point. "Anything else, Mr. Holmes? Otherwise, I shall leave you to your devices."

"One final question, Inspector. When you got here after the murder, were the curtains drawn or open?"

"Why, they were open," the detective answered, pulling on his moustache, "as they are now. We haven't touched them. 'No tampering with the evidence,' as you consulting detectives might say."

Holmes ignored the sarcasm, and Youghal went on: "The murder took place at night. When we arrived, the sun was about to rise; and when it did, obviously, even with the lights turned on, the open curtains would allow a better view of the crime scene."

Youghal paused to survey the room he and his men had already scrutinized. Predictably content with his work, he said to Holmes, "It's all quite clear, really, Mr. Holmes. The doors were locked from the inside, so Leonard must have entered through one of those French windows, picked up some bulky object—which we still have to locate—and bludgeoned his wife to death. As I say, we don't have the murder weapon yet, but I'm sure that after we find Mr. Leonard, he will enlighten us on that single, unexplained detail."

"Thank you," Holmes said. "You've been quite helpful. Please close the door on your way out."

Youghal pulled on his moustache again and seemed about to say something else. Evidently he changed his mind, for he turned, shut the door as Holmes had asked, and left the three of us alone.

I was well aware of how closely Holmes would scrutinize a murder scene. What surprised me, especially in light of Billy's weakened condition, was how eagerly the lad attempted to do so. From his position near the door, he surveyed the entire room. His eyes travelled from floor to ceiling, and then his head turned to take in the windows and walls. What he was looking for I had no idea, but as he began to step forward, I motioned for him to stand back and remain silent in order to give Holmes the opportunity to explore. I knew the ways of my friend when he was on the hunt; he needed as much freedom as possible to complete a thorough investigation, the very kind, which years of experience had taught him, the police could never seem to get right.

Sherlock Holmes removed his magnifying lens from a coat pocket and bent down on his hands and knees to examine the dark bloodspot and spatter at the centre of the blue carpet. Moments later, still on hands and knees, he crawled in a spiral direction radiating away from the central stain, keeping his lens focused on the carpet in the process. As Youghal had already indicated, thanks to the numerous windows, there was plenty of daylight to illuminate the scene.

Next, Holmes walked slowly towards the French windows that opened onto the garden. Despite the greyness of the day, there had been no recent summer rainstorms and consequently no mud in the garden to produce any random footprints nearby. Nor would one expect to find any mud on the floor. Still, Holmes persisted. At one point, he let out an "aha!" when he discovered what appeared to be a strand of light-coloured hair. Picking it up with tweezers, he carefully placed his trophy in a small envelope he had produced from his pocket. But since white-haired Terrence Leonard also lived in this house, the alleged prize seemed unimportant to me. At last Holmes rose and observed the scene in its entirety. Then he carefully walked over to the cherry-wood desk and lifted from it a foot-tall metal statue of a woman in some sort of long toga affair. Finally, he closed the heavy drapes that were currently bunched in the spaces between each of the three sets of windows.

Instantly, the room was completely enveloped in darkness. Actually, it was *almost* completely enveloped in darkness because, as soon as the curtains had been drawn, three lances of daylight, like the beams from three well-focused bull's eye lanterns, immediately shot across the room some five feet above the floor, the result of a trio of small horizontal holes inches apart in the white velvet.

"As I expected," Holmes murmured cryptically. Reopening the damaged curtain to flood the room with brightness once more, he began inspecting the wall behind the now gathered cloth at the corresponding height of the hole in the velvet. To Billy's and my great amazement, we watched Holmes discover a tiny cavity in the plaster.

Taking out a small blade from another of his pockets, Holmes pried out of the hole what looked to be a bullet. Dropping the missile into another envelope, he said enigmatically, "I *thought* there wasn't enough blood."

Holmes placed the envelope back in his coat and looked round the room once more. Apparently satisfied, he patted his pockets for reassurance. "We can go now," he said with an air of finality. "There's nothing here left to be discovered."

"But what have you learned, Mr. Holmes?" Billy asked. "What do you know that the police don't?"

"Other than the fact that Terrence Leonard's wife was *not* bludgeoned to death—that, in fact, she was shot in the head and then beaten with a small bronze statue of the Roman figure Pyramus—not much."

"Holmes!" I ejaculated. "How—?"

"Watson, *you* can see the blood stains. Certainly, there is no spatter large enough to suggest the woman had her skull stove in. And what do you make of the spots a few feet distant from the body?"

I looked round the floor where his spiral crawl had ended, but saw no blood. "There are no blood spots a few feet distant of the body," I stated.

"Precisely," he said. "When someone is bludgeoned to death, the repeated strikes create a cast-off pattern. After the initial blow that causes the victim to bleed, each successive hit will cause the weapon to pick up blood and fling it behind the killer as he prepares to strike again. Since, besides a few random drops, there is no such pattern to speak of, one must conclude that Sylvia Leonard must have been dead before the blows were administered."

"Brilliant!" Billy said.

But Holmes wasn't finished. "I imagined a bullet had done the job; the regularity of the stain at the centre of the carpet suggests she bled while lying on the floor. Because the police found no bullet in the poor lady's skull, any simpleton could conclude that there must be a bullet hole somewhere else—in the place where the bullet, after passing through her head, eventually ended up—that is, behind the bunched up folds of fabric. Since the authorities never thought to close the curtains—let alone to look for a bullet—the damage made by a single missile passing through the folds and ending up in the wall went undetected."

"Fantastic, Holmes," I offered.

"But I don't follow," Billy said. "If there was only one bullet, why are there three holes in the cloth?"

Holmes walked over to the curtain in question and pulled the fabric taut between his two hands so that the material appeared flat and the holes were readily apparent. Then he folded the velvet in such a way that he could demonstrate with the little finger of his right hand how the tiny projectile would have to penetrate three different layers, leaving a trio of holes in its wake."

"I get it now, Mr Holmes," Billy said. "But let *me* tell you about the statue. I did study classics, after all." He pointed at the small bronze figure on the table, a woman draped in robes standing under a leafy tree. "This Roman statue,"

Billy explained, "represents the woman Thisbe of Babylon. She is part of a pair. Without Pyramus, her lover, the statue has no meaning. Therefore, the mate has obviously gone missing."

"Just a moment," I said. "How do you know it's Thisbe and not some other woman from mythology?"

"Good question, Doctor." It was suddenly easy to picture Billy teaching in a Dulwich classroom. "As you can tell from the tiny clusters of fruit, the tree next to the woman is a mulberry; and according to Ovid, when Thisbe stabbed herself to death upon discovering the body of her lover Pyramus, her blood mixed with the roots of the nearby tree and turned the mulberries deep red."

"Precisely," Holmes observed.

"Like Romeo and Juliet," I mused.

"And not like Terrence and Sylvia Leonard," Holmes said. "Judging from the weight of Thisbe here, Pyramus must have made a formidable truncheon."

Billy shook his head. "I know Terrence. First shoot her? Then mash her head to pulp? He couldn't have committed this appalling atrocity; he didn't contain the rage that could produce so heinous an act. No, I'm sure he's innocent."

"When we find him, we'll know more," Holmes observed. As he spoke, he was already drawing the drapes across all of the windows in the room except the one he'd examined. "In the meantime, let us offer the police, if they choose to return, the opportunity to reach the same conclusions I did." With this pronouncement, as if about to close the final curtain on some macabre stage play, he raised his hand to the side of the velvet drapery that contained the bullet holes and dramatically pulled it across the window. Immediately, the room grew dark again. Last to exit, I closed the door, which allowed me one final look at the three tell-tale lines of light and the tiny motes of dust that were now dancing in the parallel beams.

Ω

Having secured a fellow-apiarist to look in on his bees before he'd left Sussex, Sherlock Holmes appeared determined to see the case through to its conclusion. My dear wife, on the other hand, who'd always looked slightly askance at my frequent visits to Baker Street, and who, I suspect, must have subdued some feelings of delight upon hearing of Holmes' permanent move to the South Downs in 1903, threw up her hands when she learned of his plans for an extended stay at our home. She took the opportunity to visit her cousin in Kent.

Thus, it was only Holmes and I who were in my sitting room savouring a glass of port Saturday evening when Inspector Youghal was ushered into our presence by Mrs. Meeks. His sombre mien indicated he was anything but pleased.

"Good evening, Inspector," I said. "I'd offer you some port, but your expression suggests you're here on business."

"True, Doctor Watson, but I will sit down, if you don't mind."

I offered him my favourite wing chair; Holmes and I shared the settee.

"I'm afraid I have some disturbing news," he said, drawing an official-looking paper from inside his jacket. "This is a report from the Inverness police constabulary near Loch Ness."

Holmes perked up at the name, the Scottish lake so commonly associated with rumoured monsters and fantastic sea creatures.

"What could a lake in Scotland have to do with us?" I asked.

"Watson, consider," Holmes said. "Terrence Leonard disappears; we don't know to where. The policeman in charge of the investigation arrives with news from Loch Ness. One must conclude that, for whatever the reason, that storied lake has something to do with Leonard's destination."

"His *final* destination, Mr. Holmes," Youghal said, pulling at his moustache. "As far as we can determine, Terrence Leonard left London Wednesday last, took *The Flying Scotsman* north, made his way to Inverness and then to Loch Ness, where yesterday in its murky waters he proceeded to drown himself."

Sherlock Holmes emitted what could only be described as an exhalation of disbelief. Then he bombarded the policeman with questions: "How do you know what really happened? Have they recovered the body? Was there a note? Don't you find such a suicide a bit too convenient?"

"I expected some doubt on your part, Mr. Holmes," Youghal said with a wry smile. "No, there is no body— although their lads are still looking. And there was no note. But the story satisfies Lord Steynwood; and so, I'm afraid, that is that."

"'That' is *what*?" I asked. "What actually happened to Terrence Leonard?"

Youghal tallied his points by ticking them off on his fingers. "First, a tourist boat found an empty wherry floating in the lake. Second, inside it was a small pile of clothes with Terrence Leonard's name on a label sewn inside the jacket. Third, there were small chips of rock at the bottom of the boat, leading any sensible person to conclude that Leonard must have weighted himself down in some way with large stones that he'd brought along. Fourth—and probably most important—Lord Steynwood sent one of his solicitors on the overnight train to confer with the police in Inverness today; as a result, His Lordship is convinced that Terrence Leonard, the murderer of Sylvia Leonard, has taken his own life. And, because of the powerful connections Lord Steynwood maintains with the government—including the Crown itself— we must all be in agreement that this case is closed."

"Bah!" Holmes exploded. "It is mere child's play to set a boat adrift containing some incriminating clothes and assorted pebbles."

Youghal nodded. "Yes, Mr. Holmes, you could be right. But then again, you could also be mistaken. And since we have a story that satisfies the police in Scotland as well as Lord Steynwood here in London—well, my governor has closed the books on this affair. And, therefore, so have I."

"We'll inform Billy," I said. "He'll want to know."

"Thank you, Doctor Watson. I assumed as much when I brought you and Mr. Holmes the news. I owed you that much, I expect."

We both nodded in appreciation.

"I'm sure, Mr. Holmes, that you have nothing further to tell me," Youghal said. "But even if you do believe that you have discovered something new, the Yard—with His Lordship's blessing—is no longer interested in any wild theories about what happened that night. The investigation is over."

"In that case," Holmes said with finality, "I have nothing new to report."

Youghal gave my friend a puzzled look. Clearly, Holmes had no intention of sharing with him any information about the bullet he'd pried from the wall at the scene of the murder.

After I had showed the inspector to the door, I re-entered the sitting room. Holmes was pacing the floor. "In my younger years, Watson," he said with his lips tightly drawn, "I might have endeavoured to make the trip north to follow up on these matters. But that was in my youth. Today, if Youghal is to be taken at his word, we should believe that the sordid events in this case actually occurred as he described them. Since Lord Steynwood seems to be convinced, we should, as the saying goes, 'Let sleeping dogs lie.'"

But my friend's words sounded hollow; I knew Holmes too well to accept such a verdict. His pacing began when a problem needed solving, not when he was putting the matter to rest.

"Tomorrow afternoon," he said with some finality," I shall return to my bees."

Ω

The sweltering summer sun had already begun baking London when Billy arrived early Sunday morning for

98

breakfast. Despite the intensity of the morning heat, we dined in the garden on eggs and white fish, too savoury a repast to ruin with talk of death. And yet we had to recount to Billy the story of Terrence Leonard's suicide just as Youghal had described it to us.

"Sad to say, Billy," Holmes concluded after finishing his report of Youghal's visit, "your friend is dead. According to the police, that should put an end to it."

The young man absorbed the news with furrowed brow. "I'm sorry, Mr. Holmes," he said, slowly shaking his head, "*you* can think whatever you want, but *I* can't believe Terrence killed himself. Just as I can't believe that he murdered his wife. He was too thoughtful, too refined, too sensitive."

"Sometimes," I offered, "the most sensitive of people are the least able to confront their personal demons."

"Perhaps," Billy mused and then sat silently as Mrs. Meeks brought out the coffee. The young man was perspiring, and yet he held his cup in both hands as if to keep them warm. Only after staring into the steaming brew for a good minute, did he look up. He seemed to have reached a conclusion. With the hot vapour rising before his eyes, he said softly, "I suppose that, if a detective like Sherlock Holmes can accept the outcome, who am I to say any different?"

I assumed, of course, that Holmes had *not* accepted the outcome, that he believed there really was more to these deaths than the official explanations had thus far revealed, that his immediate return to Sussex was but temporary. For a short while longer, we sat in silence again, each to his own thoughts, each contemplating the sad story of Terrence Leonard and love gone wrong. Occasionally, the trill of a visiting robin or starling broke the silence.

Yet one can stare at an empty coffee cup for just so long. At last, Holmes stood up and announced that it was time for him to collect his belongings and be off to Victoria.

Just as we were entering the house, the bell sounded at the front door. With Mrs. Meeks attending to our table in the garden and Billy nearest the entry hall, it was he who offered to unbolt the lock. I nodded, and he opened the door.

Time stopped; we three froze in our tracks.

Framed in the doorway before us was the most beautiful young woman I'd ever seen.

Her face was classical—heart-shaped with a turned up nose and high cheekbones that should have given her a haughty look but didn't. She styled her blond hair like a fairy princess, pinned in a tight chignon. But most alluring were her piercing eyes. They were narrow, almost feline, and decidedly blue, a transparent but deep, rich blue. She wore a white cotton dress accented with a long yellow shawl, neither of which could conceal her shapely form. A thin line of moisture traced the top of her upper lip. With her white-gloved hands at her side, she stood before Billy who, the closest to her—in age as well as proximity—remained still as a statue.

"Dr. Watson?" she asked him, her voice a near whisper.

The young man was speechless. One needn't have been a detective or even a doctor to tell that he was mesmerized by this vision. If truth be told, we all were. But Billy was Galahad, the knight-errant. He was Tennyson's Lancelot ready to rescue the fair Elaine.

"Dr. Watson?" she repeated, obviously puzzled by his youth.

"N-No," Billy stammered at last.

"Billy," I said, breaking into his stupor, "invite the young lady in." Perhaps she was seeking medical help—my title appeared on the brass plaque outside. Despite the clearly marked path to my surgery at the side of the house, people sometimes did approach the front door by mistake.

"Dr. Watson?" she now enquired of me as she stepped over the threshold.

"Yes, my dear," I said, feeling not unlike a giddy, young schoolboy myself, "I am Dr. John Watson." I then introduced her to Holmes and to Billy and directed her towards the sitting room.

Holmes, assuming as I did that this young woman was merely a patient gone astray, offered a quick smile and excused himself. "I have a train to catch," he explained.

"Forgive me for being so bold," the young woman said to him before he could leave the room, "but with all due respect to you other gentlemen, it is actually Mr. Sherlock Holmes, the detective, whom I've come to see. I have a problem in need of a solution, Mr. Holmes, and I have been assured that you are the man to solve it."

A look of puzzlement crossed all our faces; it was immediately followed by a wrinkle of disappointment on Billy's brow. One could read his mind: The woman's business had to do exclusively with Sherlock Holmes. Was Billy going to be asked to leave after having only just met this enchantress? For that matter, who she was and how she knew that Holmes was here were questions that I was wondering about myself.

Sherlock Holmes was not so easily distracted. "Forgive me, madam," he said, "but I am merely visiting an old friend and acquaintance. My home is in Sussex where I plan to return post-haste."

"At least allow me to introduce myself, Mr. Holmes," she countered. "My name is Elaine Sterne."

"Elaine," I heard Billy echo softly, "the fair maid of Astalot." Clearly, my allusion to Tennyson had hardly been out of place.

The damsel in question extended a gloved hand to Holmes, which he took in the most dignified manner.

"I'm married to Raphael Sterne," she said, "Raphael Sterne, the novelist."

I had heard of him, of course, one of those pretentious new writers like Eliot the American and Joyce the Irishman—Grub Street hacks whose names were bandied about for their sensationalism, but whose contributions to literature were never long-lasting. Billy grimaced, no doubt less concerned with the literary pursuits of her husband than with the notion of any husband at all.

For his part, Holmes, who'd been hoping to leave, now refocused his attention. "How can I be of help to you, Mrs. Sterne?" he asked. "For that matter, how did you know to look for me here?"

"May I sit down, Doctor?" she asked.

I indicated the wing chair.

"I trust you have no objections to my associates listening in," Holmes said. "We three have just concluded a case together."

Mrs. Sterne uttered the word "perfect," and the three of us—Billy beaming all the while at being included—took our places opposite her. *How ironic,* I thought. Following Youghal's visit yesterday and now, prepared as we were to hear this elegant woman's story today, my sitting room, unencumbered by the books, files, and test tubes always threatening to crowd us out of Baker Street, had somehow transformed itself into the consulting room of a private detective.

VI

Twenty-four hours a day somebody is running,
Somebody else is trying to catch him.
--The Long Goodbye
Raymond Chandler

"It is about the disappearance of my husband that I wish to speak to you, Mr. Holmes," our visitor said in her whispery voice.

An objective observer could easily regard Sherlock Holmes as uninvolved when a client was relating a story. Holmes might steeple his fingers and close his eyes or fiddle with his tobacco pouch and fill his pipe. All the while, of course, his mind remained riveted on the subject. But no objective observer who witnessed the three of us in attendance to Mrs. Sterne that day would have any doubt regarding which one appeared most attentive to the story told by our attractive guest.

Wide-eyed, brows knit, head nodding, Billy hung on her every word.

"He's been gone two days," she explained. "He went missing on Friday. I called on the police yesterday evening, and they told me it was too soon to start looking. They said that if I was so concerned, I should hire a private detective, someone like you, Mr. Holmes. And then a policeman in a suit—he had a rather large moustache—"

"Youghal," Billy said, eager to contribute. "Inspector Youghal."

"Yes, that was his name," she said, smiling in appreciation at the lad.

Billy straightened up, appearing all the more attentive. Perhaps another opportunity to be helpful might present itself, another opportunity to be smiled upon.

As Mrs. Sterne spoke, she began to toy with a small gold coin that hung from a thin chain at her neck. I could just discern an engraved lion and crown as part of the coin's delicate design.

She let it go in a moment and went on: "This Inspector Youghal told me that you were in town, Mr. Holmes—that, in fact, you were staying with your friend, Dr. Watson. The inspector was of the opinion that, if anyone could find my husband, it was you, so he was kind enough to furnish me with the address."

Holmes nodded as if Youghal's comment was not a compliment but a statement of fact. "Has your husband gone missing before?" Holmes asked.

Mrs. Sterne looked down and smoothed out her white dress. "Yes," she sighed. "He's a heavy drinker and occasionally would have too much and then disappear for a day or two."

"And always return, I take it," Holmes said.

"Yes," she replied, returning his gaze.

"So why, pray tell, are you so concerned on this occasion? Why not simply await his arrival as you have done in the past?"

"Because Rafe has been so upset lately. He's been working on a novel about explorers in darkest Africa and hit an obstacle. He can't seem to finish; his publisher has been after him."

"I'm not surprised," Billy concurred. "I'm a bit of a writer too. I know exactly what you're talking about. And the drinking when things start to go badly."

"Not all writers need follow such a course," I reminded Billy. Consuming alcohol had no place in the instructions on writing that I'd offered the lad.

"And yet this time I don't believe that drinking is Rafe's only problem," Mrs. Sterne said. "There's something else beyond the writing and the drinking that's bothering him, and I don't know what it is."

"I see," said Holmes, steepling his fingers in his characteristic fashion. "And where has he gone in the past during his previous disappearances?"

"I've read some of his books," Billy interrupted. "*Wild Seas* was a bit overdone, but generally engaging."

Mrs. Sterne smiled at him again, exactly the response I'm sure Billy was hoping for, her blue eyes now flashing despite her concern.

"Quite," Holmes muttered, obviously annoyed by Billy's digression that required Holmes to repeat the question. "Just where has he taken himself when he's gone off in the past, Mrs. Sterne?"

"That's the thing, Mr. Holmes. He doesn't tell me. I believe he attends a secluded clinic where like-minded, unfortunate public figures go in the attempt to rid themselves of their intemperate ways. The so-called doctors who run these places charge lots of money to keep the lofty reputations of their patients intact and their locations secret. In the case of writers, the reading audience is very fickle. Authors can be shunned if their vices become too public."

"Oscar Wilde," Billy contributed again. "His dear friend 'Bosie'—Lord Alfred Douglas—used to be the editor of *The Academy*, one of the publications in which my writing appears."

"And why have you not made enquiries at this clinic itself?" Holmes asked, again ignoring Billy's diversion.

"As I've already said, I don't know where it is, who its proprietor is, or even how much poor Rafe is being made to pay. That is why I have come to you."

Sherlock Holmes leaned back in the settee. "Have you no idea at all, no clues?"

"I once heard Rafe talking about a 'Dr. V'," she said. "But whether such a man is even a doctor is beyond my ken."

"My directory of medical doctors in London should help us solve this mystery," I volunteered. And excusing myself, I hurried to my consulting room, located the volume in question, and returned within a few moments to our attractive visitor and the others. Old fool that I am, I found myself thinking all the while I was gone that perhaps *I* could be the lucky one to eliminate the damsel's distress . . . .

As I had expected, a quick survey of the names revealed a handful of physicians whose surnames—assuming that was what we were looking for—began with the letter V. But they were all respected Harley Street doctors, certainly no one running a clandestine operation like the one described by Mrs. Sterne.

Sherlock Holmes looked into the deep blue eyes of the lovely face before him. Then he rose, and the rest of us also stood.

"Mrs. Sterne," he said, "I will try to find your husband. It is the least I can do to help so concerned a wife."

And so young and beautiful a client, I couldn't help thinking. It had been much more a challenge for the older Mrs. Chandler to engage my friend's services.

"Oh, thank you, Mr. Holmes," said our visitor. "I'm staying at the Langham. Ordinarily, we live in Marlow."

Holmes and I exchanged glances. His faced perceptibly darkened. Could it have been more than coincidence that had brought another citizen of Marlow to our attention?

"Where the Leonards live—lived," Billy said to no one in particular.

"Yes, poor Sylvia," Mrs. Sterne said. "I met her once or twice, you see. What a terrible end."

"I knew her husband," Billy volunteered. "Killed her and then himself, they say." He felt compelled to add, "though I still don't believe it"—as if such a sentiment would mean anything to Mrs. Sterne,

In fact, Mrs. Sterne shook her head as if physically disconnecting herself from the Leonards' misfortune. "Please find my husband, Mr. Holmes," she implored.

My friend offered a quick, reassuring smile, and Mrs. Sterne allowed Billy to lead her through the door and out into the sunlight. I followed them to the doorway where I could see her four-wheeler at the kerb. With its brass trim flashing in the sunlight, it looked like some grand medieval coach awaiting the beautiful princess.

As the carriage was making its way down the road, Holmes joined me at the door.

"Quite an attractive young lady," I observed.

Holmes didn't reply.

"How will you find this Dr. V, then?" I asked.

He offered another one of those abrupt smiles. "I have my ways, Watson, as you know so well."

Clearly, Holmes' return to Sussex was going to be deferred.

Ω

On Monday morning I attended to my patients and by noon was able to return to my sitting room. Much to my surprise, a uniformed police constable was sitting on the settee engaged in conversation with Holmes. The policeman's helmet was resting on the end table. Both men rose when I entered, and I gave Holmes a quizzical glance.

"You don't know PC Ruggles then?" Holmes asked in response to my cluelessness. "PC Sam Ruggles?"

"No," I said slowly. "Should I?" He was a tall young man with red hair who seemed to be suppressing a grin.

"Wot, Doc," he said, "Don't remember old Sammy then?"

Perhaps I did see something familiar in the face—the lop-sided smile, the slightly crooked teeth, the protruding ears.

"One of the Baker Street Irregulars," Holmes prodded. "When Wiggins matriculated, Sammy took over the lead. He and his mates helped us on many an occasion."

"Of—of course," I said with some hesitation.

"Sam here," Holmes explained, "became the head boy just before I retired to the Downs. But we kept in touch, and his detecting skills seemed perfectly suited to gain him admission to the constabulary. A word to Inspector Gregson helped grease the wheels."

"Sammy, so good to see you," I chortled, slapping him on the back. Maybe I did recall that same half-smile on the face of a much younger lad. "I'll have Mrs. Meeks bring in some sandwiches."

"Thank you all the same, Dr. Watson," Sam said, "but I must be off. I have work to do for Mr. Holmes." With that, he put on his helmet, offered a good-bye salute, and exited.

Yet again I gave Holmes a quizzical look.

"Ah, Watson. How do the French put it? *'Plus ça change* . . . . The more things change, the more they stay the same.' As a society, we are now well into the twentieth century, and still the poor boys gather in various London neighbourhoods looking for food and money. You and I employed their skills some twenty years ago, and yet here they are still. Different boys; same talents. Sam has been looking out for the current Baker Street lot and helping to steer them in the right direction. I gave him a few pounds to scatter amongst them in hopes that they can help us find this den for inebriated toffs and the Dr. V who runs it."

"Capital!"

"Yes," Holmes said. "Now we simply await the results. Actually, those sandwiches you mentioned a few moments ago sound like just the thing."

A loud knocking suddenly penetrated the house. Mrs. Meeks, responding to its urgency, pulled open the front door.

Billy bolted into the sitting room, holding out a piece of paper. "A letter from Terrence Leonard!" he announced. "Posted just before he died."

A letter from a dead man. Stunned, Holmes and I said nothing.

"Letters from the dead create their own silence," Billy observed. He would often encapsulate in a single sentence some much grander philosophy. It was a guileful way he had, employing a compact comment to deflate his pompous-sounding wisdom, and yet it was wisdom just the same.

His observation hung over us as we stood waiting for him to share the contents of this post from beyond the grave.

"There's no date or salutation," he said and then began to read the hand-written letter: *"I'm staring out my window in a small hotel in Inverness, the Scottish highlands out in the distance. I'm about to make the short journey to Loch Ness during which I plan to drop this letter through the slot in a post box and send it on its way to you. I am including some money because I know it can do you some good. There's no point in taking it with me and certainly no point in leaving it behind with my clothes. Don't question its purpose; it's a kind of apology for all the trouble I've caused you and a small way of thanking you for looking out for me as you have.*

"With all that you've no doubt heard about me and my wife, you've probably already made up your mind about the kind of person you think I am. Who really knows what anyone is capable of? I certainly don't. Who can even remember each and every pain one has inflicted on another? Who would even want to try? I just can't believe myself capable of turning her into what was lying there on the floor. But it really doesn't

matter any more. Her father was always kind to me, and he deserves consideration now. He has his own life to live, and here I am disgusted with mine. Sylvia didn't destroy me; I did it to myself. Whatever else one may say, she will never know the terror of growing old. With all her father's money, she deserved a better life than the sour one she had.

"There is nothing heroic or noble in my act; it is all sordid and grim.

"Enjoy the money. All I ask is that one day soon you take yourself to the Crown and Eagle and drink a gin gimlet for me. Then forget this whole mess. As for me, I'm going for a cruise in Loch Ness.

"A fifty-pound note was inside the envelope," Billy concluded.

Holmes took the curling paper from the lad and, with the aid of his magnifying lens, examined it from all angles. His careful scrutiny revealed nothing beyond its having been written in common black ink on common-enough stationery bearing the name of a small hotel in Inverness. Billy confirmed that the handwriting looked like Leonard's and that the envelope, which Billy in his haste had left in his room, displayed the appropriate stamp and markings. In short, Holmes concluded, the letter seemed exactly what it appeared to be: a true communication from Terrence Leonard written just before he took his own life.

Billy had no clever comment, no grand pronouncement, no simple wisdom—only the silence he had described before, the silence evoked by a letter from the dead.

Ω

Later that Monday afternoon, despite a hot summer sun that sent many a Londoner to the wooden benches and green lawns of the city's numerous parks, Holmes, Billy, and I entered a small turning off Holborn. Each of us sported lightweight linen suits, so that we might appear to be three gentlemen out for a summer constitutional. But we all knew that we were on a mission of liberation.

I had expected an establishment catering to the well-heeled to be much closer to Harley Street than to Holborn, but in just a few hours the Baker Street Irregulars had found a small number of illicit sanatoria near Holborn—easily recognized by the bars on their upper-storey windows, not an inviting architectural *accoutrement* for the well-to-do patrons of Harley Street. In just such an institution, run by a Doctor Vering (consistent with the "Dr. V" Mrs. Sterne had told us of), the boys had learned of a writer who had been admitted a few days before. One small grimy lad in particular led us to the proximity of the building; and Holmes, stopping him before we made the turn from Holborn, thanked him with a couple of coins.

Just beyond the turning, not a hundred feet from the ominous tall wooden doors at the front of the grey edifice, we congregated to receive our instructions from Holmes. I was to be the diversion. Holmes' plan had me, as a medical man, entering the establishment to find Dr. Vering and then to engage him in conversation however I could. The possibility of sending a patient for treatment to his institution seemed as good a ruse as any. At the same time, Holmes and Billy would slip in by a side entrance and, with the aid of a photograph of our quarry, canvass the upper three storeys for any sign of Raphael Sterne. Once we had completed our initial assignments, we would reconnoitre in this same spot; the actual rescue would occur later. Our adventure had all the qualities of a covert military stratagem.

According to plan, we went off in our appointed directions. Holmes and Billy casually strolled round the corner of the building while I strode boldly up the three steps that led to the entrance. I took a deep breath and marched inside.

Almost immediately, a brown-haired, stoop-shouldered man scurried over to intercept me.

"Dr. Vering, I presume?"

No, he was merely an attendant. Schulhof, by name.

"Velcome," he began politely enough. He spoke with the guttural sounds of a German accent, and he pronounced his w's like v's. "It is my pleasure to velcome you here. Today is busy, but—"

"I am a doctor," I interrupted, "and I would like to know more about the workings of your regimen. In point of fact, I am most reluctant to send any of my patients to a hospital where the sick are hemmed in by *bars*." This last word I voiced forcefully, hoping that the combination of my loudness and scepticism would attract attention.

"I understand," Schulhof said calmly. "But some patients require such treatment, you see."

"Certainly not those suffering from alcohol abuse. They must make up much of your clientele. I should imagine," I dared to add, "that their forced confinement might be of some interest to the police."

As we spoke, my voice continued to rise, and a heavy little man with a pointed grey beard strode quickly in our direction. As I had hoped, he turned out to be Dr. Vering himself.

I took as much time as I could to introduce myself, drawing out the history of my medical career in the process. I spoke of my degree from the University of London, the staff work in surgery I performed at St. Bartholomew's Hospital, my training with the Army Medical Department at Netley, my field service in Afghanistan, and my current practice in Queen Anne Street. Only after I'd completed this chronicle did I resume my criticism of Dr. Vering's program.

"Ah," the man smiled, "my dear Dr. Watson. If you don't mind my saying so, despite your distinguished background, it is obvious that the path you have chosen in our noble profession has not provided you many dealings with the rich. For them, health is not the only issue. Such people hope to keep their names out of prying newspapers and salacious periodicals. Some of our patients come here for relaxation, but many are here to seek the means of divorcing themselves from 'demon-rum.' The admittedly high fees they pay enable us to employ the attendants that keep their names away from Fleet Street."

"And the barred windows?"

"Tosh," he said with a flick of his hand. "A subtle way of telling our patients that we're serious about their cures. We minister to their minds as well as to their bodies."

From a distance, I heard a muted hammering, perhaps an unhappy resident pounding on a locked door.

Dr. Vering must have heard the sound as well, for he found it necessary to terminate our discussion. In the interest of delay, I tried to raise additional questions, and to his credit, he tried to exit politely. But when Dr. Vering realized that I would not be dismissed so readily, he motioned for two muscular chaps in white coats to help escort me out. Reluctantly, I retreated through the doors and back out into the sun, hoping all the while that my *charade* had given Holmes and Billy enough time to locate Raphael Sterne.

Once outside, I returned to our previous meeting place with what I hoped to be a gait as far from suspicious-looking as possible. Holmes and Billy had not yet arrived, and I spent an anxious few minutes until I saw them exiting the same side door through which they had entered.

"Mr. Holmes was brilliant!" Billy beamed once we were reunited. "He has these tiny metal tools that he used to unlock the door. And I thought that getting inside was going to be difficult . . . ."

"But what did you discover?" I asked.

"We went up to the third floor," Holmes reported, "and Billy and I each took a side of the hallway. We checked every room until we found poor Sterne. He's strapped to a bed, looking as if he hasn't shaved in days or slept very much. Tonight, when it's dark, we'll come back and get him out."

Billy smiled broadly. "Let me tell Mrs. Sterne that we found him. She'll appreciate the message."

"Billy," I cautioned, "she's a married woman."

"More to the point," Holmes said, "let's not tell her anything until we've actually secured the man. In the meantime, gentlemen, dinner at Rules might be in order." And rubbing his hands in anticipation, he walked off down the road in search of a hansom or growler that would take the three of us to Covent Garden.

Ω

I was appointed sentry. Despite the day's heat, the night had turned cold, and the black sky added an appropriately dark backdrop not only to the heavens but also to the illegality of our mission. After dinner, we returned to Queen Anne Street to change into darker clothing and then returned to Dr. Vering's sanatorium. From where I was standing, I could see Holmes, dressed for the hunt in deerstalker cap and Inverness cape, leading Billy to the now familiar side entrance of the building. The small road that I was left to observe ran perpendicular to Holborn and presented little traffic, pedestrian or otherwise. A large motor-car was parked a good distance down the road, but I could make out nothing inside; and certainly, at this late hour, no one would be entering the grounds of the institution itself. My responsibility was to engage in conversation anyone approaching the side-door that Holmes and Billy had previously entered. In short, I was to keep out unwanted visitors.

How well I remember the wait on that mid-summer's night. The stillness of the empty road did nothing to blanket my anxieties. After all, Holmes and Billy were illicitly entering a business establishment, and Scotland Yard—no matter how much (or, perhaps, because) Holmes had helped them in the past—would like nothing better than to assert some authority over their rival detective. There was little to see in the darkness, and sounds and smells dominated. The receding echo of footfalls on Holborn; the plaintive mews of a cat in search of food; the acrid stink of horse dung and petrol—all co-mingled into an ominous oppression that seemed to last a very long time.

In reality, it was no more than a half-hour when I heard the scrape of a window sash opening on the second storey, one level below those barred windows behind which patients like Sterne were held. At first, the wall appeared dark; but then despite the shadows, I could discern what looked like a long light-coloured rope poking its way out the unlit window and left to dangle some five feet above the ground. I was put in mind of the fearsome "speckled band" that (despite Billy's earlier scepticism) had descended a similar cable so many years before on its mission of death. Yet on this occasion, even in the darkness, I could see Billy's face peering out the opening and then his arm motioning me to come closer.

Once I reached the wall, I discovered that the rope was actually a series of white bed sheets tied together end-to-end. Gazing upward, I espied a figure clad only in grey hospital pyjamas, a man I correctly took to be Raphael Sterne, throw a leg over the window sill—in the process, accidentally sending a dark leather slipper down on my head. He took hold of the makeshift line and lowered himself to its end, dropping the final five feet to the pavement. Breathing heavily, the dishevelled writer stood next to me, trying unsuccessfully to stand up straight. Despite his obvious discomfort, he did have the presence of mind to gesture for his recently departed slipper. With his palm outstretched like that, there was a certain humility about him, while his drawn face, tousled black hair, and vacant stare suggested the ordeal he'd so recently endured.

In another instant, Billy was dropping down next to me, and Holmes was quickly exiting the same side-door he had entered earlier.

Billy, who'd appropriated a wool blanket from inside the sanatorium, draped it over the tall, but still bent frame of Raphael Sterne. By the time Holmes caught up with us, Sterne, Billy and I were already striding towards Holborn.

"An excellent plan, Watson, if I do say so myself," Holmes beamed. "Of course, we did have some improvising to do. Once Billy and I recovered Mr. Sterne, we ran down the back stairs to the first floor, but the three of us couldn't all go out of the front or side exits because there were too many watchful eyes for three culprits to evade. Since only the third floor had barred windows, the second provided an exit. We found the sheets in a storage closet, and I left it to the younger men to utilize them. I returned to the ground floor, knocked over a potted plant near the front exit to create a distraction, and made it out through the side-door when the aides on duty went off to investigate."

"Well done, Holmes," I said as we turned onto Holborn.

"But, Watson, my apologies," he replied. "Allow me to introduce you to the noted novelist Mr. Raphael Sterne."

Though we'd met less formally over the missing slipper, I shook hands with the haggard writer, impressed that in his worn-out condition he had still been able to negotiate a rope made of bed linen. At the same time, Holmes was replacing the blanket covering Sterne's pyjamas with his own cape. Perhaps Holmes had brought it along with just such a need in mind.

"Sterne was being held until he or someone else agreed to pay Vering one hundred pounds," Holmes explained as he signalled a passing cab. "Otherwise, Vering in some devious manner threatened to make known to the public the exact nature of Sterne's illness. Fifty pounds was the original fee— itself a form of blackmail or extortion. When Sterne refused to pay, the price immediately doubled. But now Sterne's free and sober—I should imagine Vering should be thanked for that development—and it's time to get him safely home."

The road from which we'd initially emerged appeared quiet. But now traffic was all round us, and Holmes had no problem hailing a hansom. Most probably, no one at the institute had yet discovered Sterne's disappearance, but Holmes was taking no chances. As soon as the hansom pulled up next to us, Holmes opened the door and bundled Billy and Sterne inside. Holmes and I would take another cab, for Holmes had reasoned that Billy would appreciate returning the liberated husband to the man's beautiful wife on his own. While I agreed with Holmes' insight, I wasn't as sure of his judgement. Billy seemed too eager to complete the assignment. Perhaps his intent was simply to embellish his own role in helping free Raphael Sterne, but the look of irritation he flashed at Sterne when Holmes mentioned the word "wife" had all the hallmarks of jealousy. Whatever the motive, Billy and his charge were immediately off to the Langham where Mrs. Sterne was staying.

Despite this minor triangle, Holmes and I relished the success of our mission. Indeed, I was feeling quite pleased with myself as we flagged a cab to take the two of us back to Queen Anne Street.

"Quite a good night's work, eh, Holmes?" I said, as our journey home began.

"I would like to agree with you, Watson, but—" Rather than finishing the sentence, he proceeded to lean out of the side window to get a look behind our hansom. Once he'd resumed his seat, he concluded, "—the large black Daimler, which earlier had been parked near Dr. Vering's institution, is now following us."

"A black Daimler?" I said, recalling the large, dark motor-car I myself had seen stopped at some distance from the sanatorium.

"A coincidence, Holmes. Who could have known we were there?"

"At this moment, my dear fellow, I cannot answer that question. But I do know that the Daimler was stopped by the kerb near Vering's when we arrived this afternoon and that it followed us to and from Rules."

We sat in silence for the rest of our journey, the sharp clatter of the horse's hooves and the throaty purr of the Daimler's motor the only sounds intruding on our thoughts.

Soon enough Holmes and I stood before my front door watching the Daimler approach. It was a large, closed car with a fluted front grill and a hawk-nosed driver in dark livery at the wheel. As it motored past us and drove on down the road, one could almost believe that whoever was ensconced in the passenger seat had no interest in our simple comings and goings.

But, of course, whoever might have thought so naively would have been gravely mistaken.

Daniel D. Victor

VII

She gave me a smile I could feel in my hip pocket.
--Raymond Chandler,
Farewell, My Lovely

"To the memory of Terrence Leonard," Billy said, raising his glass.

"Terrence Leonard," Holmes and I echoed simultaneously.

At Billy's invitation the three of us had agreed to meet the next evening in the Crown and Eagle. Our purpose was to fulfil the request Terrence had made in his missive to Billy: to have a drink in Terrence's honour at his favourite pub. It was a Tuesday night in the business district; the bankers and barristers and clerks had finished their after-work drinks and gone home. Besides a couple of gentlemen at the back who were silently hoisting pints, the bar and tables were empty. Silent and still, the taproom seemed a fitting place to hold a memorial.

We began as Terrence had requested, drinking gin gimlets.

"Ah, yes," Holmes intoned after a long pull, "the gin gimlet. Supposedly named for Sir Thomas Gimlette, Surgeon General, KCB. He had the clever idea of mixing spirits with lime juice to ward off scurvy aboard battleships."

123

"Then here's to Sir Thomas," Billy said, raising his glass again.

"Sir Thomas," Holmes and I said and sipped some more.

"A bit too sweet for my taste," Holmes observed. "The things we do to honour our dead. May Terrence Leonard rest in peace."

The lugubrious thought hovered above us for a few quiet moments.

"Speaking of Terrence Leonard," Billy said, "I—" A sudden ring of laughter from the men behind us distracted him.

"Let's talk about the living, shall we, Billy?" I suggested, taking advantage of the opportunity to express my concerns. "Raphael Sterne. You gave him quite a nasty look when you climbed into the hansom last night."

Billy's face flushed. "I realize that we had just saved him from the evil Dr. Vering," he said, "but I know too many pretentious writers like Sterne—genteel types who spend more time on their grooming than they do on their writing. I'm sure he's never felt the bitterness of poverty or the heartache of lost love or even the joy of reverie in the countryside. He's just a literary hack."

"Surely, you're being prejudicial," I said, fortifying myself with more gin.

"His latest book—*Wild Seas*?" Billy continued, "a lot of action, but nothing to suggest that he knows how his characters *feel*. To writers like him, literary composition is a business and not something to interfere with the fancy parties they get invited to. What's more—"

"This criticism of yours," Holmes interrupted, "it wouldn't have anything to do with your attraction to the enchanting Mrs. Sterne?"

The young man blushed and stared into his glass. It seemed to require only Holmes' prod and another sip of the gimlet to render Billy rhapsodic. "I can't get her out of my mind," he said sheepishly. "Her golden hair. Those blue eyes—cornflower blue, they are—and those long, pale lashes . . . ."

His own eyes seemed trained on some vision neither Holmes nor I could locate; indeed, he seemed to be talking more to himself than to us.

"Her smile, " he continued, "it's so tender, so pure—it's paralyzing. She reminds me of a fairy princess. When she walks, she sways like a rose in the wind. When she speaks, her voice is music." He blushed again. "Someday I'll write a poem about her: 'Elaine the fair, Elaine the lovable'—although that's Tennyson, actually."

"Be careful, young man," I cautioned. "You may have a talent with words; but, as you said yourself, *this* Elaine, unlike Tennyson's, is a married woman—married, if I may remind you, to a successful and celebrated author—your opinion notwithstanding."

"Author?" Billy's eyebrows arched. "I already told you he's a hack! Raphael Sterne is a genteel dilettante! He lacks any of the passion—fanaticism, if you will—that the true artist must extract from life to produce great art. I've often thought that the English writer is—or is not—a gentleman *first* and a writer *second*. Why, I've seen better writing than Sterne's at Dulwich College."

"Methinks the lad doth protest too much," Holmes observed.

"You know, Mr. Holmes," Billy countered, "I hadn't thought of it before, but now that you raise the question, I do believe that my opinion of Sterne is worthy of dissemination. I should publish my thoughts. I'll write an article for *The Academy*." He paused a moment to consider; then his eyes lit up. "I'll call it 'The Genteel Artist.' I won't identify Sterne by name—I wouldn't want to harm his wife—but at the very least, I will posit an antidote to your implied charge of jealousy."

"Well done, Holmes," I said, "you've ignited the creative spark."

"To the creative spark," Billy answered, and we all took another swallow.

"Actually, Mr. Holmes," Billy observed, "what I was going to say about Sterne before you brought up his wife—" (my friend bowed his head in false modesty) —"was that, when I took Sterne home last night, he told me that he'd heard of me—that my name had been mentioned to him by Terrence Leonard."

"Really," Holmes mused, setting down his glass. "Sterne knew Leonard? But not so strange really when we remember that Mrs. Sterne herself told us she'd met Leonard's wife."

I too recalled that fact from our initial conversation with Mrs. Sterne.

"The fact is," Billy went on, "the Sternes and Leonards were neighbours. At least, they lived in the same town, Marlow—if not in the same neighbourhoods. Sterne said that some time or another Terrence had described to him those two occasions I'd helped Terrence when I'd found him so drunk he could hardly stand up."

Holmes finished his drink and put down the glass. "We're devoting too much attention to the wrong people," he said. "We came here to remember Terrence Leonard, not the Sternes. I suggest it is time to go." About to push away from the table, he added, "Besides, Billy, I shouldn't think that you'd have any cause to see Mrs. Sterne in the future."

"Actually," Billy said with what I could only describe as a self-satisfied grin, "Mrs. Sterne herself asked me if I might come out to their home in Marlow tomorrow evening. She's invited some people for a drinks-party and hoped I could attend. She wants someone to help keep an eye on her husband. She'd really like to know what's been upsetting him so much. We know he's been a heavy drinker; but as she tells it, this time he went off in the *middle* of a novel, which he's never done before. She also says he's been much quicker to anger. Since I helped him escape from Dr. Vering, she'd like me to do more if I can."

"And the disdain for her husband that you spoke of but minutes ago?" Holmes asked.

"Working with him is the price I'm willing to pay to see his wife again. I will do my utmost to remain an objective observer."

Such circumlocution was too much for me. I was about to protest Billy's obsession with this woman when he announced that Holmes and I might attend the party as well: "'Bring along your two friends,' she wrote me. I didn't tell you because I didn't think you'd be interested. Now, seeing your concern—"

"I'm afraid I have some other matters to attend to," Holmes said. "But, Watson, *you* might have a go at it. That way you could be sure that Billy's behaviour remains true to the Dulwich code."

"Sorry," I said, uncertain whether Holmes was being sarcastic. "I have my patients to think about." If Holmes wasn't going to take responsibility for his former page, I certainly would not. Billy was a grown man. It wasn't up to me to be his chaperone.

In fact, Billy had already planned his trip. The following afternoon he would travel to Marlow, attend the social gathering, and return on the last train to London. His job, as he had told us, was to support Raphael Sterne on the novelist's journey back to health.

"If I may," Holmes said to Billy, "since you are determined to go, I'd like to request an additional task."

"Anything," Billy offered.

"You are a writer. Keep notes on what transpires. Describe in detail your experiences in Marlow. Although our dealings with Raphael Sterne appear to be finished, don't fail to record any matters of concern."

"Much like my assignment with that ghostly hound on the Grimpen Mire, eh, Holmes?" I said, recalling my friend's request for letters to him in London while I stayed at Baskerville Hall those many years ago.

"Precisely," Holmes said. "Except that Billy can bring his report to us himself rather than having to post it."

"Mr. Holmes," Billy said, "you flatter me with the request. I'll see you upon my return then."

We finished our drinks and exited the pub in different directions; Billy wandered off to Bloomsbury; Holmes and I, back to Queen Anne Street. Personally, I felt a trifle tipsy. But however much the world was spinning, my vision was clear enough so that on this occasion, I too, as well as Holmes, noticed the black Daimler parked across the road. It was slow to start up; perhaps its occupant was confused over which direction to take, Billy's or ours. But soon we could hear the deep purring sound as its engine sparked into life, and it began to move slowly behind Holmes and me. After we'd secured a cab, the Daimler continued to follow us all the way to my house, departing from us there in much the same manner it had displayed on the earlier occasion. The hawk-nosed driver we saw once more; its passenger remained a mystery.

Ω

I interrupt my narration at this point to include the written report of Billy the page regarding his experiences in Marlow that Wednesday and Thursday. I include two caveats: first, Billy's style is significantly less formal than that of his more disciplined literary essays, which he contributed to publications like *The Academy* and *The Alleynian*. Second, his observations are psychologically—dare I say, shockingly—frank. Billy's informal style, probably developed from his experiences as a journalist, seemed to have instilled in him a greater confidence the more often he utilized it, resulting in his many candid observations, revealing thoughts, and disturbingly explicit details. Although I personally attribute Billy's openness to his American roots, I leave it to the wisdom of my perspicacious readers to determine the true motivations for the account that follows.

Ω

Wednesday morning,
26 July 1911

To Mr. Holmes and Dr. Watson:
Forgive me if I sound like a faux näif, *but with no characters in the drama yet to appear, I thought I might sharpen my pen by describing the lie of the land. I commence my short journey to Marlow on a wonderfully warm summer's day. Indeed, the sunlight penetrating the railway carriage makes it easy to read the words I set down on paper. I can only hope such light will just as successfully illuminate the rest of the events I encounter. And yet one can't forget that bright sunshine also renders stains the more clearly.*

As I'm sure you know, the town of Marlow lies some thirty miles west of London. From what I've read, its major claim to distinction is that the poet Shelley lived there some time in the early nineteenth century. Since I've never actually been there, I reckoned that it wouldn't be too difficult to reach. But when I arrived beneath the vaulted glass roof of Paddington at mid-morning, I discovered that the short journey actually requires three trains.

A lurch followed by a gentle swaying alerts me to the start of my trip. The first and longest leg ends at Maidenhead. After escaping London, we roll west across steel bridges and stone viaducts, travel the brief but monotonous route through the high embankments and sharp cuttings of the verdant English countryside, and finally cross a low bridge of bricked arches that not only spans the sparkling Thames but also marks the immediate approach to Maidenhead.

For some reason, the bridge itself looks strangely familiar, and then suddenly I recall Mr. Hose's lecture back at Dulwich about Turner's ghostly painting, Rain, Steam, and Speed, *which depicts this very crossing. Perhaps you've seen the work; it hangs in the National Gallery as part of the Turner Bequest. Whatever grand design Turner may have intended with those ethereal orange and white swirls of mist and vapour that envelop so much of the canvas, the bridge and train remain readily perceptible; and I now believe, as we rattle along the rails of the G.W.R., that Mr. Hose got it right when, ignoring the eerie constructs or the lofty interpretations, he simply called the landscape Turner's "tribute to the Great Western Railway."*

The second part of the journey runs from Maidenhead to Bourne End. The railway leaves Maidenhead and follows the sweep of the Thames to the north. In the afternoon sun you get a vivid view of the river winding its way like a sinuous serpent through the green hills of Buckinghamshire. On a small plateau above looms Cliveden House, that majestic architectural playground of the rich, its Italianate terraces lording over the pedestrian rail and river traffic below. I've never seen it before, but who hasn't heard of the celebrated place or its famous history? Such fantastic homes require lots of maintenance, of course; and over the years its one-time wealthy owners frequently ran out of money. Then Cliveden

House would change hands as quickly as the church plate on which no one wants to leave a donation. Funny, in that respect, it's a lot like Lord Steynwood's estate, Idyllic Vale. *Terrence liked that name. He said it fit since the so-called aristocrats whom he had run into over there could accurately be described as the "idle rich."*

To have heard Terrence tell it, Lord Steynwood himself was anything but idle. Apparently, His Lordship's money came from sugar, which he had imported from the Colonies somewhere in the Caribbean. Lord Steynwood, so the story goes, bought Idyllic Vale *from a turn-of-the-century tobacco importer who had needed more cash. His Lordship completed his marriage of wealth and influence when he spent much of his fortune on a string of important newspapers.*

Now, as we all know, the man born Lucius Ward stands before us as one of the preeminent powerbrokers of our age. Which means, of course, that once everyone came to believe that Terrence Leonard had killed Lord Steynwood's older daughter, His Lordship could—and, I'm convinced, did—make certain that that was how the story would remain. Blame it on the husband. That way, gossip about Lord Steynwood's daughter could be contained.

Lord Steynwood possessed the capability to make people believe Terrence killed her. Lord Steynwood—or his people—could have caught up with Terrence and forced him to confess. From what Terrence used to tell me, I have no doubt Lord Steynwood had the means necessary to convince Terrence that, from the moment Sylvia died, Terrence's life would no longer be worth living. In short, the suicide of Sylvia's husband has been most convenient for Lord Steynwood.

The train whistle hoots. It might be in derision of my conspiratorial theory. But then again, it might be an underscoring. What it really does is announce our arrival at Bourne End just across the river.

As we roll into the station, an ominous great tower of steam billows from the unseen locomotive that will complete the final leg of the journey from London to Marlow. But soon I have to laugh. This "powerful" locomotive turns out to be nothing more than a small, green, cylindrical tank engine with the white numerals 522 on the front—altogether more fit to model for a child's toy than for delivering all-important people on their all-important errands. Only now does a fellow passenger inform me that you complete the third part of the journey to Marlow on a small railway so slow that with great affection the locals have nicknamed it "The Marlow Donkey." When it finally completes the just-under three miles to Marlow, the little engine trumpets a loud blast of its whistle to announce its arrival, a grand gesture from so meagre a source.

(The rest of this account I shall complete during my return to London.)

Ω

Who could have predicted that an evening begun so calmly could end with so much drama?

Red-brick buildings trimmed in white line Marlow's High Street. With a deep-blue sky as background, yesterday presented a beautiful afternoon for a walk to my destination. A leisurely stroll past a number of intersecting roads brought me to a turning just off West Street. On that picturesque lane canopied by arching boughs stands the unique cottage of Elaine and Raphael Sterne. Its disjointed storeys, its bricks in varying colours of honey and red, and its steep mansard roof make it one of the craziest-looking houses I've ever seen, an ill-matched puzzle whose pieces have been jammed together. Studying its overlapping lines long enough could make you dizzy.

To be honest though, gentlemen, it really wasn't my critical reaction to some off-kilter building that was quickening my pulse, but rather the thought of seeing the fair Elaine.

The invitation had encouraged casual attire, and I was dressed in boater and light linen. Some twenty people were already milling about when I arrived. Upon my entrance, a stuffed shirt in a dinner jacket took my hat, and I immediately snatched a flute of champagne from a silver tray carried by a cute, sparkling-eyed little maid in a crisp black-and-white uniform. In the drawing room, Raphael Sterne, the man of the hour, was mixing with several genteel characters bedecked in flowery waistcoats and iridescent ascots—a bouquet of humanity, you might say. They seemed caught up in some dilettantish banter; but upon noticing my appearance, Sterne began madly waving his arms in a frantic effort to motion me over.

Unfortunately, I must now report that, despite our noble attempt to save Raphael Sterne from the hellish den that his drinking had led him to, it was quite obvious from his stentorian pronouncements and raucous laughter, not to mention his bloodshot eyes and swaying gait, that he'd been hitting the bottle again. I reckon that you have about as much chance of separating a drunk from his alcohol as detaching a priest from his collar.

Then Elaine stepped into view.

Obviously, she had heard her husband's loud voice, and now she walked—perhaps "glided" is a more precise term—towards us. Tonight, her golden hair tumbled to her shoulders. She was dressed in midnight blue, a fabulous low-cut chiffon fabric that, without its black underpinning, you could almost see through, the gold-coin necklace seeming to float on the swell of her breasts. Yet her piercing eyes of cornflower blue expressed an annoyance I hadn't seen before. On the previous occasions we had met, her primary emotion had been one of concern. Tonight she was full of wrath. Even in anger, with her eyes narrowed and her mouth pursed, she reigned magnificent.

"Rafe," she said to her husband, "you've had quite enough."

Stashing his glass on the oak sideboard behind him, he held out his empty hands. "But I'm not drinking anything, my dear."

"You know exactly what I mean," she charged.

"I was merely about to welcome our friend—" and here he actually embraced me "—to the writers' district."

Fortunately, he let me go after a moment, about as long as I could tolerate the stink of his alcoholic breath.

"Oh," he went on, "perhaps you don't know why I call it the 'writers' district."

I presumed that the term must have had some connection to Shelley, but I shook my head at his reference.

"You see?" Sterne said, staring Elaine down. *"Actually,"* *he went on to explain, "Shelley and his wife lived in Albion House not far from here. It's where she finished* Frankenstein. *And Shelley's friend, Thomas Love Peacock, the novelist, lived just round the corner in West Street.* I *live here, and now* you've *arrived—a contributor to* The Academy *and to* The Gazette *if I'm not mistaken."*

"And The Spectator, *" I added.*

An effete young man sporting round eyeglasses and a long white cigarette in an ebony holder regarded me for an uncomfortable moment.

"Chandler, is it?" he asked, "R.T. Chandler, the poet?"

"Guilty as charged," I quipped.

The flock of swells shared a round of laughter, though I couldn't be sure whether they were laughing at my wit—or at my poetic aspirations.

"And what are you working on now, my dear boy?" asked a young dandy. Sporting a shock of black hair and a red ascot, he couldn't have been much older than I.

"A couple of essays," I answered. "One deals with the ever-increasing tolerance of readers towards heroes. The commonplace reader doesn't concern himself with the breeding of his heroes any more. He demands only that these heroes can distinguish themselves in some way. Those are the heroes I call 'remarkable.'"

Raised eyebrows greeted my explanation—as if they'd originally deemed me incapable of formulating so erudite a thesis.

"But lately," I went on, "I've become even more interested in the nature of the writers themselves, the kind of writers that some people call artists"—here I turned to gaze in particular at the man with the long cigarette holder—"but whom critics like me call 'literary fops.'"

The group scattered as if iced water had been dumped on them. All but Sterne. He took the opportunity to retrieve the tall, narrow glass he had attempted to hide. After a long pull, he said, "You sound a bit irked with the current state of belles letters."

"Only with some of its inhabitants." In his intoxicated state, I realized, he would never conclude that I might be referring to him.

Indeed, he took up only my earlier reference and lifted his glass to mine. "Here's to 'remarkable heroes'—like you and Sherlock Holmes and Dr. Watson—would they were here—who rescued me from the villainous Dr. Vering." And then he gulped down the rest of his champagne.

At that moment a new couple entered the fray: a portly, middle-aged man with ginger hair and a grizzled beard accompanied by a handsome, raven-haired young woman.

"Dr. and Mrs. Goring," the stuffed shirt announced.

So this was Cora, Sylvia Leonard's younger sister, accompanied by the very doctor Lord Steynwood had called after the fact to administer to Terrence Leonard's murdered wife. Marlow seemed to be a small world.

As the Gorings steered in our direction, Sterne observed through clenched teeth, "Of course, Elaine had to invite him. She's always inventing some bloody reason to see the bastard."

Goring's eyes travelled over Elaine' body, and a broad smile splashed across his face.

"You stay away from my wife!" Sterne suddenly shouted.

Shocked surprise eclipsed the doctor's smile; his wife clutched his arm.

"Now, Rafe," Dr. Goring said. "You know you have these silly fantasies." He spoke slowly, as if talking to a child. "You really must control yourself."

It was instructive to watch the two women during this exchange. Elaine's face turned red, not out of embarrassment—or so it seemed to me--but out of anger. Cora's brow furrowed, as if she was annoyed; and, tugging at her husband's arm, she pulled him across the room towards some other couples, who were still marking the tense encounter with open mouths.

"I told you we shouldn't have come," Cora whispered to the doctor as they passed.

At the same time, Elaine was cornering her husband. "Rafe," she commanded, "that's enough! This is supposed to be a celebration of your return to society. Let's not have you fall apart all over again." And with a hand at his elbow, she steered him away from the crowd and seated him on a damask sofa.

Eyes closed, Sterne sank into the pillows. At the same time, his wife walked across the room where she stood quite alone for a few moments. It was, I realized, the perfect opportunity for me to approach her. Maybe she recognized the mien of the hunter as I dared to close in, for she began nervously twisting the gold doubloon at her neck. And yet she allowed me to guide her through the open French windows, which I closed behind us, and out onto the balcony. The balcony overlooks a garden, which has been carved out of the small hill just below the ground floor of the oddly-shaped house. The sun had disappeared, but the warmth of the day still lingered. We faced the darkness together as a train whistle echoed through the night. It must have been the Marlow Donkey announcing its latest arrival.

Elaine leaned towards me, her deep-blue gaze piercing my soul like a sword. "I owe you many thanks," she whispered.

I took her face in my hands and, shop-worn Galahad that I am, kissed her hard on the lips.

I know what I was hoping for; I didn't anticipate what I got. She stood there looking blankly at me. I grabbed her shoulders and, holding her at arm's length, tried without any luck to penetrate her stare. She reacted the way the tree greets the woodcutter. I let her go, and she, clutching the small doubloon, walked slowly back into the house.

I followed soon after, trying to understand what had just happened. She was a married woman, after all, and yet she hadn't pushed me away. On the other hand, she hadn't taken me in her arms either, as I was so eagerly anticipating.

I'd already missed the last train, and I was in no hurry to leave. With nowhere to go, I sat dumbly by, watching others collect their wraps from a hired footman and make their way out the front door. Sterne himself had quit the scene much earlier. I hadn't seen him go up the stairs, but I was well aware of his absence. For her part, Elaine was seeing the Gorings off; all the while she never looked at me. By midnight,

I seemed to be the only guest remaining, and with no alternative but to say good-bye, I stood up.

Suddenly, a cry echoed from the deserted garden like the caw of a crow in an empty field.

"Help me!" a quavering voice called out. Despite the tremulous tone, I recognized it immediately as belonging to Raphael Sterne.

With Elaine right behind me, I ran out into the night and down to the garden. I stood just below the balcony that Elaine and I had occupied a short time before, but now the warm air held a clamminess that I hadn't felt earlier, a cold clamminess that attached itself to my collar. Despite the night's heat, icy fingers clutched at my neck.

Even in the darkness, I could distinguish Sterne sprawled out at the foot of a thick hedgerow. As I approached him, I saw blood dripping from the right side of his head. I grabbed my handkerchief and pressed it against what appeared to be a cut above his temple. I hoped I could stop the bleeding.

"God!" Elaine exploded in a mixture of pity and disgust—and I might be exaggerating the pity

Since she clearly wanted nothing to do with this mess, I guessed that I would come in handy after all. I hurried back into the house, found the hired butler who'd taken my hat when I'd arrived and motioned him out to the garden. "Let's get him upstairs," I said when he got over the shock of seeing his employer collapsed in the bushes. With poor Rafe barely able to drape his arms around our shoulders, the two of us staggered into the house half dragging the semi-conscious writer.

Between us, we managed to get Sterne up the staircase and into his bedroom. With its padded chairs of Russia-leather, elaborate mirrors, tall mahogany secretary's desk, and gold-banded fountain pens, it was easy to see that the room also served as the writer's study.

At the same time we were struggling to get the poor fellow into his bed, Elaine was dismissing the servants she'd hired for the evening. Mrs. Jenkins, her housekeeper, brought us some white towels, and I cleaned the wound—a small cut above his right ear, as it turned out—and then the butler and I prepared the patient for sleep with a pair of blue silk pyjamas. When Sterne looked settled, we left the room.

I found Elaine sitting at the dining room table with a small glass of port.

"What do you suppose happened to him?" I asked.

"What's the phrase?" she said with a quick, embarrassed laugh. "Falling down drunk? He must have tripped and hit his head."

"Or maybe," I suggested half-heartedly, "somebody hit him."

"Don't look at me," *she said. "I wasn't in the vicinity."*

At least she and I were talking again.

That was when the gunshot roared through the house. The report so startled Elaine that she overturned her glass. The red wine pooled on the white linen like a bloodstain.

This time it was Elaine who took the lead, running up the stairs in fear and desperation to reach her stricken husband.

Bathed in electric light, Raphael Sterne lay diagonally across the bed in a sea of twisted sheets, right hand dangling over the edge, mere inches from where a pistol lay on the floor.

All that was missing from this Grand Guignol *was the blood.*

But you see, gentlemen, there was no blood because there was no wound. What there was in actuality was a bullet hole in the ceiling above the bed. It seemed quite apparent to Elaine and me that the poor fool lying before us had tried to blow his head off and missed. Talk about ineptitude! If I ever entertained such an act, I would bloody well be sure to aim more carefully.

Elaine was shooing away the maid and the butler who had arrived at the doorway together. Although Elaine was blocking the door, I'm certain they could see the entire ugly scene reflected in the mirror. In the flesh, they could see me picking up the pistol. I know very little about guns; this one seemed pretty large.

"Where did this come from?" I asked as we got her husband settled back in his bed.

"He kept it over there." She pointed across the room to the mahogany secretary's desk. Just below the closed writing table, the top drawer gaped open.

Trying on the role of detective, I walked over to the desk. At the front right corner of the open drawer, I could see spots of blood. My fingers told me it was still sticky, but certainly not wet enough to be related to the immediate shooting. The open drawer was probably the place where Sterne had struck his head before ultimately stumbling out some back door and ending up in the bushes where we'd found

142

him. I placed the gun back in the drawer, which I pushed closed.

Elaine sat down on the bed next to her husband. I took one of the padded leather chairs. Although Sterne was breathing deeply, he was still awake, occasionally searching the room from beneath half-closed eyes. But she was looking at me. Only at me.

"I'm hoping you'll spend the night," she whispered, clutching the small coin at her neck. I'm doing my best to care for him, but he's pushing me to the brink. I'd greatly appreciate your help." The cornflower blue eyes began to well up with tears. "I'm sorry about how I reacted before. You and your friends have been a great help. You deserve better."

I raised my eyebrows. Her meaning could be taken in different ways.

"Of course," I said. "I'd be happy to stay."

She stood and took both my hands. An electric jolt coursed through me.

"Thank you," she breathed. "We want to get Rafe back on his feet as quickly as we can. Then grasping the small doubloon, she left me standing by her husband's bedside. At the door, she turned back with a lingering stare. "I'll have the maid make up the room two doors down the hallway. Mine is the first door—in case there's an emergency. But could you wait with him until he falls asleep? I'm exhausted."

I nodded, and she, brushing at a misplaced lock of golden hair, glided out of the room.

Sterne's deep breathing soon transformed into the stentorian rasps of sleep, and I rose from the chair and began the trek to my awaiting room. With no sliver of light showing at Elaine's threshold, I could tell her room was dark. But as I was passing the door, it swung open a few inches; and after deliberating for a moment, I pushed it open wider and walked in.

In the moonlight, I could make out Elaine's form near the window. Immediately, I caught my breath. At first glance, she appeared naked. But then I realized she was wearing a wispy sort of nightgown, which, thanks to the light behind her, I could see right through.

It didn't matter much because, as soon as I entered the room, she untied a bow and let the fabric fall to the floor. Then she held out her arms.

Stark images of another nude woman suddenly seared my brain. This one was sitting in a teakwood chair surrounded by windows covered with paper. A fetching smile seemed aimed in my direction.

Elaine had opened her door for me; that much was obvious. And when she stretched out her arms, it was I she was summoning. And yet, though I couldn't decipher the sound, it wasn't my name she was murmuring.

"Your husband's asleep now," I said as I put my arms around her. Her body trembled at my touch, and I embraced her all the tighter.

"I knew you'd come back to me," she whispered. "I've been waiting years for you. Shut the door."

I did as instructed. I also did as instructed when she told me to lay her on the bed. I cradled her yielding form in my arms and carried her to the awaiting sheets, their whiteness glowing pale-blue in the moonlight. Here was the moment I had imagined when I'd first seen her, her soft flesh quivering under my fingers, her dark lips parting in expectation.

But just as I was about to envelop her, I heard the doorknob turn. Jumping up, I raced to the door and opened it—only to see Mrs. Jenkins scurrying back down the stairs.

I shut the door and looked down at Elaine. She was whimpering and mumbling at the same time, sounds I couldn't distinguish except to feel that they were not meant for me.

But the spell had been broken.

I quietly left her room and padded off to mine.

Ω

The next morning, sunlight pierced the chintz curtains in my bedroom as if they hadn't been there. In the daylight something had changed in my thinking. Maybe it was the way Elaine's mood had altered when she wanted my help. First, I hardly existed; then, I could do no wrong.

I dressed and walked downstairs. Elaine Sterne, clad in white cotton, greeted me at the breakfast table—as though what had occurred last night in her bedroom had never happened. As though she hadn't seen me in weeks. As though her memory had gone blank.

"I put the gun back in the desk," I told her as she stared at the buttered toast on her plate. "But you really shouldn't leave him alone with it."

"Gun?" she said, her large blue-eyes now staring at me. "Oh, yes," she recovered. "I remember now," and she twisted the golden doubloon on the chain encircling her sculpted neck. I leaned towards her and took hold of the coin

still attached to the chain. The movement brought her face close to mine. I could feel her sweet breath on my lips. Fingering the coin, I examined it more carefully now: it bore a patriotic design, vaguely militaristic—a lion engraved on a crown atop some sort of rosette.

"I'm glad Rafe is sleeping," she whispered in my ear. "I hope he'll be fine from now on."

"I wish I could believe you," I said, "but the way you've been reacting to your husband—and to me, for that matter—makes me think that you're hoping to appear concerned—when maybe you're really not."

She leaned back, forcing me to release the doubloon or snap the chain. "That is a beastly thing to say," she hissed, eyes narrowing. Then she rose and walked out, leaving me sitting alone in the middle of the room.

Who is she? I wanted to know. But to be honest, gentlemen, at that instant, what I really wanted was to leave this so-called "writers' district" and get back to London.

Immediately.

VIII

There ain't no clean way to make a hundred million bucks.
-- Raymond Chandler
The Long Goodbye

Lord Steynwood's invitation arrived after I had completed my consultations that Friday morning, but before I had the chance to see Billy or to read his scandalous report. Lord Steynwood's communication was addressed to Holmes and me, bidding our attendance at tea that same afternoon at *Idyllic Vale*. A chauffeur would be sent to meet us by 3:00 at Bourne End if we could manage to arrange our railway transportation to that point.

I was sharing the invitation with Holmes, who had joined me in the sitting room, when both of us heard what by now had become the familiar hum of a motor-car engine. I am certainly no authority on the differences among automobiles, but the Daimler's soft purr was most distinctive, and Holmes and I peered through a front window to see what the vehicle and whoever was inside might be up to on this occasion.

This instance was clearly different. The car had stopped, and its front door stood agape. As we watched, the driver, the same hawk-nosed young man in dark livery we had espied before, stepped out and marched to the side door, which he opened for its occupant. It was the long white moustache we recognized first, and I must say that Holmes and I were both quite surprised to see the sinister figure who emerged: tall, dark, elderly, clad in formal dress with black cape, top hat, and ebony walking stick. In the brightness of the morning sun, his attire looked almost comical. Nodding at the driver who remained at attention by the Daimler, he strode determinedly to my front entrance. With the silver handle of his stick, he rapped loudly on the wooden door. No sooner had Mrs. Meeks opened it than he saw Holmes and me at the nearby window and, brushing boldly past her, marched directly for us. Despite the years, the vengeful visage was clearly recognizable. We stood face to face with Colonel Sebastian Moran, the prime disciple of the man Holmes used to refer to as the Napoleon of Crime, the late Professor James Moriarty. In point of fact, Holmes had once labelled Moran "the second most dangerous man in London."

"I received word that you'd been released from prison," Holmes said to him coolly, "but I had no idea you would come calling."

It was obvious that Moran had aged. His defiant stance was now slightly stooped; the moustache was whiter, and the scowling furrows more deeply entrenched. Yet I could easily discern that thin, projecting nose and those cruel, blue eyes that had fixed on us almost two decades before when Moran had been apprehended in his abortive attempt to assassinate Sherlock Holmes. As the world will remember, Holmes had placed a wax effigy of himself in our Baker Street window; and from the empty house across the road, Moran had believed he was taking deadly aim with his air rifle at Holmes himself. It was the very tableau I had reprimanded Billy for falsely resurrecting in his version of Holmes' recovery of the Mazarin Stone.

Moran removed his hat and placed it carefully on a nearby chair. His high, bald forehead reflected the sunlight from the window. "The police," he growled, "have warned me to keep my distance, Mr. Holmes. As if I fear anything the police have to say." He punctuated his derision with a snort.

"H-how did you contrive to be released?" I managed to ask.

"Dr. Watson, the ever faithful lapdog," he spat out. "Even you should know that, if one has the talented stable of solicitors and barristers that I do, one cannot stay imprisoned for long on the charge of shooting at a wax figure."

"But Ronald Adair," I said, referring to an actual murder he'd been charged with and that I had reported in "The Empty House." "You killed him."

"Circumstantial evidence, I'm afraid, Doctor," Moran said, his lined face managing a smirk.

"As I heard it," Holmes said, "you were offered a pardon if you agreed to serve with Her Majesty's forces in South Africa. As much as I may detest you, Moran, I cannot minimize your talents as a marksman. Couple that with your lack of scruples about killing, and you make quite the lethal weapon."

Moran offered another twisted smile. "Rather than suffer a string of humiliating new trials, it is true that the Crown granted me a pardon in exchange for services rendered against the Boers—which, incidentally, brings me to the matter at hand."

"Do tell," Holmes said. "I've wondered why you've been following us in so obvious a manner."

"The truth is, Holmes, I've taken rather a keen interest in your meddling into the suicide of Terrence Leonard."

I was shocked, to say the least. For better of for worse, I thought we'd put that case to rest; obviously, Moran had not. *What could Billy's friend Terrence have to do with the rogue before us?* I wondered. *Could the Boer War serve as some sort of common denominator since both Leonard and Moran had fought for Her Majesty in South Africa?*

"The poor man is dead," Holmes observed. "A suicide in Loch Ness."

"True," Moran said. "Let Terrence Leonard remain at peace. That's what I've come to tell you." Leaning on the stick, which he held in his right hand, he now pointed the long index finger of his left in my friend's face. "Stop your nosing about, Mr. Sherlock Holmes. And tell that bloody writer friend of yours to leave the story alone as well."

"Billy," I half-whispered.

"*All* of you," Moran said, now waving his stick in a semi-circle before him. "Let the matter drop. Or"—quick as a flash, he shifted the stick to his left hand, whipped the handle from its base with the other, and jabbed a long, thin rapier under the chin of Sherlock Holmes—"or the dead of Loch Ness may gain some *new* company. You and I, Holmes, are not done yet," he snarled. "One day I shall get level with you."

Speech done, he replaced the slender blade. Then, abruptly seizing his hat, he pivoted on his heel like the military man he had been, marched out of the house, and returned to his place in the waiting vehicle. The chauffeur with the aquiline nose slammed the door shut, and in a moment the Daimler sped off.

I managed to exhale only after the motor-car had vanished down the road.

"Come, Watson," Holmes said. "It's time to prepare for our journey to Marlow."

"Holmes," I sputtered, aghast at how easily he could dismiss the melodrama that had just unfolded.

"To Marlow," he repeated with grim determination.

Ω

Although I could not so easily put from my mind the image of that fine blade poised at Holmes' throat, we had an appointment to keep. We boarded the G.W.R. at Paddington, changed trains at Maidenhead, and were met by chauffeur and silver Rolls Royce at East Bourne. The road we followed descended in the direction of the Thames along the natural curves of the verdant hillocks. Soon it straightened out and then narrowed, and we found ourselves on a long roadway lined on either side by grey poplars. Their branches formed a thin canopy that caused the sunlight to flicker as we motored along. In a few minutes, we were able to discern the end of the roadway and our ultimate destination— *Idyllic Vale*, the grand house of Lord Steynwood.

From the distance, I could make out only a large, simple square structure of honey-colour stone whose crenulated front wall was topped with a small tower and cupola. But as we got closer, I could more easily see the three storeys of windows, including the dormers below the roof. A black wreath hanging on one of the two massive doors of dark oak seemed the only sign of mourning for Lord Steynwood's daughter.

The automobile, crunching its way up the curved gravel drive, came to a stop before the entrance and immediately a footman in formal livery marched out to help us exit the car. Once inside the house, I could see that the building was laid out as a kind of square frame whose massive walls surrounded the angular designs of a geometrically-designed brick courtyard and green garden. The magnificent display formed an altogether appropriate representation of a man with the wealth of Lord Steynwood.

A footman took our coats, and the butler ushered us through the main hallway, which itself stood two storeys high, and into the sitting room. Holmes and I seated ourselves in two matching leather wing chairs beside one of the largest hearths I had ever seen. Despite the warmth of the day, a fire blazed within; had it not, one could walk comfortably within the dimensions of that cavernous fireplace. No sooner had we sat down, however, than we had to rise, for His Lordship was just entering the room.

"Unless you are in need of refreshment, gentlemen," he said, motioning for us to sit, "I suggest we skip the tea and concern ourselves with the matter at hand. No sense in wasting time."

"I believe I can safely speak for Dr. Watson," Holmes replied, "when I say that we never thought of this meeting as a social gathering. Pray, let us proceed with the business at hand."

Lord Steynwood seated himself in a small, wooden bow-back chair. It had been placed next to a butler's table on which stood a humidor full of cigars. Holmes and I declined the offer, but His Lordship extracted one and snipped off an end. He lit it with a match from an inside pocket of his frock coat.

As he manipulated the match, I had the opportunity to study the celebrated publisher. A modern man, he seemed somehow anachronistic. He was slight of stature with dark features although his black hair, parted in the middle, was going grey at the sides. In addition, his old-fashioned side-whiskers, which extended down to his thin lips, had also gone grey. Most obvious—and what added most to the sense of his coming from an earlier era—was the *pince-nez* that adorned his nose. They forced him to tilt his head back when he spoke to us. I felt like an object under constant examination.

A white cat peered out from behind a leather couch and padded in a straight line to His Lordship. With a small leap, it curled in his lap and allowed him to stroke its neck.

After a few moments of such petting, Lord Steynwood exhaled a large cloud of pungent smoke, filling the room with the sweet smell of costly tobacco. "It may be a cliché, gentlemen," he said at last, "but time is indeed money. Shall we get to the point?"

"Yes," said Holmes, showing great restraint in not pointing out that it was Lord Steynwood himself who had been delaying the conversation. "I'm quite interested to learn whatever it is that led Your Lordship to summon us. Of course, I have my own theories."

"I'm sure you do, sir, and that is part of the problem. Simply put, I'd like you to stop meddling in my affairs."

Holmes smiled. "That's the second time today I've been warned to stay away. And as in the first instance, I wasn't aware that the matters I and my associates have recently been–as you so kindly put it—'meddling in' are any part of your affairs."

"Come now, Mr. Holmes," he said, exhaling another cloud of smoke. "I know what kind of activities you are involved in. Solving crimes and so forth. I make it my business to find out what's going on in my world, and I know that Terrence Leonard, the murderer of my daughter Sylvia, came to Dr. Watson for help after fleeing the scene of his beastly work. What's more, I know that the blackguard fled to Inverness and graciously dispatched himself in some act of contrition—but not before sending a letter to another one of your so-called associates."

"And which associate is that?" Holmes asked.

"The associate you persist in calling Billy the page— the associate, I don't have to remind you, who maintains direct contact with a man quite familiar to my late daughter."

"And who might that man be?" I dared to ask.

"Raphael Sterne, Dr. Watson. Raphael Sterne." He spoke the name with disgust. "Said to be a writer of some repute. 'Infamy,' might be a better term. Judging from what I know of his alcoholic nature, probably not one whose work I would choose to read. Or publish. For that matter, not the type of man I would have reckoned for a pal of yours, Mr. Holmes."

Sherlock Holmes smiled. "Not a 'pal', Lord Steynwood."

His Lordship let out a derisive laugh.

"I don't expect my opinions to change your mind, Lord Steynwood," Holmes said, "but I don't believe for an instant that Terrence Leonard actually beat your daughter to death."

I expected some sort of surprise from Lord Steynwood in reaction to Holmes's divergent conclusion. But His Lordship continued stroking the white cat. At the same time, he emitted another cloud of smoke, this one containing some accidental rings, which the cat tracked with its green eyes as the circles floated upward. "I am a trifle disappointed," he said, "that a detective with the reputation of Sherlock Holmes did not discover that my poor Sylvia was actually shot first and then bludgeoned."

"With all due respect," Holmes said, "my 'associates'—as you like to call them—can testify that I too came to that conclusion, the very same conclusion that helped convince me Terrence Leonard is innocent."

Lord Steynwood stared at Holmes through those little glasses at the end of his nose.

"What's more," Holmes said, "I personally never sought contact with Mr. Sterne—although you probably know that already as well. It was his wife who asked me to help her find him in some disreputable institution where he was supposedly ridding himself of his addiction to alcohol. I will confess, however, that until you just revealed it to me, I was not aware of any sort of relationship between Raphael Sterne and your older daughter."

Lord Steynwood crossed a leg, careful not to upset the cat. "'Relationship' is just the word. Perhaps you think me callous, gentlemen, in speaking so coldly of my daughter. But

I've been forced to. Sylvia was not the most discerning of women. Especially when it came to the men in her life. Without a mother to guide her, she conducted numerous unwise liaisons. Raising concerns about blackmail, unwanted pregnancies and the like, she was driving me to distraction. Then she brought round this Leonard fellow, an apparently decent chap unfortunately disfigured in heroic service to the Queen. So when Sylvia actually fell in love with someone whose only major vice appeared to be pauperism, I encouraged her to marry him. Surely, Mr. Holmes, you can see the hope I had of a marriage to this Terrence Leonard bringing some sort of conclusion to her wild ways. But then the young man became a drunk, you see. And, later, worse."

For a moment behind the *pince-nez*, the man's dark eyes appeared to moisten.

"Yet surely," Holmes said, "a young man who deserves better than to be falsely remembered as the killer of his wife."

"See here, Holmes," Lord Steynwood barked, his face reddening, his eyes bulging. "I'm not used to being contradicted." At the vehemence of his tone, the cat leaped to the floor and disappeared behind a tufted ottoman on the other side of the room.

Fearful for His Lordship's condition, I gestured that he calm himself. "Is this a display of anger, My Lord?" the medical man inside of me questioned. "It can't be good for your health."

"When I am truly angry, Dr. Watson," he said coldly, "you won't have to ask."

A silence descended. Lord Steynwood puffed on his cigar, its end glowing bright red; Holmes steepled his long fingers, never taking his eyes off the man. I looked back and forth from one to the other.

"Terrence shot her with her own gun," Lord Steynwood said. "At least, it has gone missing. Had that been the end of it, a competent barrister might have convinced a jury that the gun had gone off in Leonard's attempt to take it from his suicidal wife. If he had come to me then, I might have been able to help him. But after all that other business—snatching away the gun, running to you, Dr. Watson—it was obvious that he had no chance for exculpation, and so he fled to Scotland."

Holmes nodded. I knew he was impressed that Lord Steynwood had revealed his knowledge of the gunshot, a fact which the police had yet to discover. His Lordship's knowledge about the gun itself, however, was simply inaccurate; and Holmes seemed in no hurry to correct him.

"He had to escape," Lord Steynwood continued. "I told him so when he finally did telephone me. I told him I didn't want to know where he was; he should jolly-well find someone else to aid him. I absolutely did not want to suffer a trial that might bring up all sorts of personal titbits about my daughter, my family, and my personal dealings. When I heard of his death, I can't say that I was unhappy."

"Of course, you weren't unhappy," Holmes said. "But only if you believe that Terrence Leonard killed your daughter."

Lord Steynwood sighed. Holding the cigar upright in front of his face, he pondered its glowing tip and then slowly shook his head. "Are you not understanding what I'm saying, Mr. Holmes? You do not have a reputation for being thick-headed." He uncrossed his legs and spoke directly to my friend. "I don't give a fig who murdered my daughter. My wife died when Sylvia was quite young, and I took the responsibility of raising her and her younger sister. I hired the best governesses one can find. But I am a private man who owns powerful newspapers that can topple governments. My business must remain private."

"With all due respect," I said, mustering my courage, "in a democracy—"

"Bah!" he ejaculated. "I'm speaking of the real world, Dr. Watson, not the fictive one of novels and short stories in which the good citizens live happily ever after and the miscreants face justice. In the real world, there is no good and evil; there is just power. A few misguided politicians may think they have it, but the most intelligent people in government know that they do not. The truly powerful, Doctor, don't have to question. They simply watch the results of their domination."

"Bravo," said Holmes. "A speech worthy of Professor Moriarty himself."

Lord Steynwood smiled. "You're beginning to understand after all."

Holmes and I exchanged glances.

"Gentlemen, I expect your investigation to cease. I'm an old-fashioned man who does things in old-fashioned ways. What can I offer you to seal our agreement? Money—or simply an honourable drink?"

"May I remind you," Holmes countered, "that it was *you* who asked *us* here. We came seeking nothing; yet we leave with new information. We have only just recently met the alcoholic Mr. Sterne, and today do we discover that—with all due respect—he was but one of many who'd had relationships with your daughter Sylvia. Now if we should happen to learn that he too has some history of violence . . . ." Holmes' voice trailed off, as if to dramatize his final thought: "Your Lordship, the memory of Terrence Leonard deserves more than a simple dismissal."

Lord Steynwood stood up. Despite his denials, his red face told us how much he was seething inside. "Mr. Holmes, you should return to the South Downs." It was more of an order than a suggestion. "Otherwise, you might find your beloved cottage and all its bees in someone else's hands. Or you, Doctor," he said, turning his eyes on me, "you could find yourself without a medical practice."

"Along with bullets in our heads?" Holmes prodded. "Like your daughter?"

"I don't operate in that manner, Mr. Holmes. Nor do I bribe or physically threaten the people I do business with. I don't have to."

He extended his hand to signal that our time with him had ended. The footman arrived with our coats, and then the butler showed Holmes and me out.

"First Moran, now Lord Steynwood," I said to Holmes as soon as the door closed behind us. "I marvel at all this concern over a relative unknown like Terrence Leonard."

"We seem to be entering deep waters, old fellow," Holmes said. They were the only words he spoke during our entire trek back to London.

When we finally arrived at Queen Anne Street, Mrs. Meeks handed us Billy's report of his trip to Marlow; he had left it with her in our absence. In retrospect, I can only marvel at what an ominous day it had been. If the threats from Colonel Moran and Lord Steynwood weren't bad enough, we would now take turns perusing Billy's disturbing observations. Not only would we read his lurid account of Raphael Sterne and the writer's familiarity with guns, but also the scandalous record of Billy's most intimate thoughts regarding the man's wife—thoughts that, as far as I was concerned, he would have been better off keeping to himself.

Daniel D. Victor

IX

When I split an infinitive, God damn it, I split it so it will stay split.
--Raymond Chandler
Letter to the *Atlantic Monthly*

I had never visited Billy's digs in the cheap boarding
house just north of Russell Square. As he told it, for 9s 6d per
week, he got a small room; a cold, greasy breakfast left on a
metal tray outside his door; and—if he were in the vicinity and
actually wanted to face such a bill of fare—ale, bread, and
cheese for lunch. On warm days like the present, the room
seemed intolerably hot; during the winter, I imagine one never
removed one's coat. Through the half-open doors of a large
wardrobe, I did catch a glimpse of Billy's highly prized and
smartly tailored suit. But such care seemed the exception to
the rule. The white paint was cracking on most of the
moulding; and the wallpaper, which might once have been
burgundy in colour and floral in pattern, curled down in so
many places that someone had taken to tacking it back into
position. On a makeshift bookcase, an empty vodka bottle
stood next to a stack of dog-eared books; and a half-full bottle
stood on the floor next to the bed. In such a place, a writer like
Billy could fancy himself quite the Bohemian. Here he was
free to drink, free to smoke, free—dare I say—to avoid the
judgements of his mother. Despite all his independence,
however, I could easily understand why Billy preferred visiting

Holmes and me in what he must have regarded as my palatial estate rather than inviting us to see him confined in his run-down artist's garret.

And yet the night after reading his so-called report, I braved all the obstacles he had warned me about in trying to keep me away.

"Beware those white spectres of Russell Square," he wrote in response to my telegram announcing my intention to visit.

By "white spectres," I assume he meant the pale but harmless souls begging for food who invade so many of our parks until the police run them off. He said I might be driven mad by the violinist in his block who played Bach much too loud or by the two "wooden butterflies," who considered themselves actors and would occupy the stairwell to share their sad fates with anyone who had the misfortune to be in their vicinity. A strange cast of ne'er-do-wells, perhaps, but in light of the miscreants and rogues I had encountered in my adventures with Sherlock Holmes, certainly not menacing enough to thwart my intentions. Come what may, Billy was going to hear from me that he had to conform to the proprietary rules of society—especially in print. No list of vagabonds was going to put me off.

"Fortunately," I said to him as soon as I entered his room, "only Holmes and I have read these intimate details of your profligate night in Marlow." I tossed his report onto a small wooden table. The pages landed next to a red-and-black chessboard whose pieces appeared *in medias res*.

"Be careful," Billy cautioned, checking that all the chessmen remained in their proper positions. "I'm in the midst of a game against myself."

"A game against yourself," I echoed. "How well that sums you up: on the one hand, an Alleynian from Dulwich College, a product of Mr. Gilkes' upstanding moral code; on the other, one of those salacious writers who must tell everything—your licentious desires, your libidinous acts. Or so you sound in that report of yours."

"You mean the report that expresses my *feelings*?"

"Your *feelings*," I snorted. "In your poetry, you seem able enough to present feelings of a more uplifting nature. What happened to all those lofty ideals? Your romantic poems display a sense of discipline, of self-control. Personally, I have yet to be convinced that sexual activity need ever be promoted in print." It was warm enough for me to mop my brow, and I sat down on the only seat available, a wooden desk-chair.

"But, Dr. Watson," Billy said with what I can only describe as a smirk, "you and Mr. Holmes wanted a thorough account of what went on—or so you said. Aren't my personal thoughts and observations part of that charge?"

It is true that, when I'd told Holmes I was going to share with the author himself my outrage over such indiscretions, Holmes had simply filled his briar and smiled. "You're too easily offended, old fellow," he'd said. "Knowing the nature of the lens through which we are viewing enables us to make the necessary adjustments for evaluating the results. We need to be aware of those occasions when Billy was roused by passion, when his judgement might have been marred. Watson, you of all people know the effects of overpowering emotion. If we are aware of Billy's instability, we can better judge the validity of his conclusions."

I couldn't disagree, but I still had to admit my discomfort at reading of Billy's presence in the *boudoir* of a married—let alone, nude—woman. "After all," I said to Billy, "who knows where, despite our best efforts to guard it, such a manuscript might end up?"

"Who knows where, indeed?" Billy said, picking up a straight-stemmed briar that looked much like one of Holmes' favourite pipes. "Perhaps in the kind of magazine the French call *avant-garde*. I could be touted as the British Flaubert or even de Sade—daring writers who weren't afraid to break moulds."

"*Avant-garde*," "Flaubert," "de Sade"—*here were the results of Billy's stay in Paris*, I thought as he held a flame over the tobacco. And yet he did have a point. If I was honest in recognizing my own prejudices, I should be able to compliment him on what I thought the young writer had done well. He had kept us apprised not only of Raphael Sterne's condition but also of the writer's recklessness with firearms. In addition, Billy had noted a possible connection between Sterne and Sylvia's younger sister Cora, a connection that, if true, would help corroborate the accusations made by Lord Steynwood against the novelist.

"I did like your detail," I offered almost by way of apology, "especially the depiction of the drawer in Sterne's mahogany desk. A much more accurate description than that early account of the Mazarin Stone you concocted. And as much as I hate to encourage you, that bit about the moonlight was most engaging. For that matter, I have always liked your ear for dialogue, and some of your metaphors are quite clever. That quip about separating a priest from his collar? Most apt."

Billy recognized my intent to support him. "Thank you, Dr. Watson. Your compliments mean a lot to me. Mr. Hope and Mr. Hose remain my favourite school masters, but you will always be my literary mentor."

I blushed in response; it is always pleasing to be appreciated. Nonetheless, after regaining my composure, I still felt compelled to make the distinction between his writings and his actions. "However well you reported the goings-on in Marlow," I said, "I really must caution you once again to keep away from the Sternes, especially Mrs. Sterne. I can't state it any more strongly."

Puffing away on his briar when I left, Billy gave no indication that my words of caution would be heeded.

Ω

And so matters stood for the next few months. Reinstituting the plans he'd made before Mrs. Sterne's dramatic arrival at my doorstep in July, Sherlock Holmes journeyed back to Sussex and his bees. "I'm afraid, Watson," he said before leaving, "that we haven't heard the last of those people in Marlow. But we must let matters percolate on their own."

Billy continued to fashion his literary career. As he had threatened, he shifted his emphasis during that summer of 1911 from romantic poetry to a scoffing prose. Thanks to the critical perspective he'd sharpened in Marlow, the acerbic tone of his new compositions did not surprise me. His disgust with pretentious writers in general and with Raphael Sterne in particular could be inferred from the titles of his articles that appeared in *The Academy* later that year: "The Genteel Artist" in late August, "The Remarkable Hero" a few weeks later, and "The Literary Fop" in the fall. "Commonplace readers," as Billy liked to term his audience, might think of his criticisms in the abstract; I, of course, recognized Sterne as his target.

So pleased was I with his success at publication that I hoped to compliment Billy personally. One cool night in early November I visited him in Bloomsbury for a second time. As in our previous meeting, he sat on his bed and offered me the desk chair. Billy appreciated my praise but, like many a young writer before him, observed that his was a limited success. Writing had earned him but a pittance, his continued confinement in so seedy a room obvious proof of his questionable achievement.

"Look at this place," he cried, waving his arms at his shabby surroundings. "Maybe I should move back with my mother."

"Don't be ridiculous," I said rather quickly. "You're gaining a reputation, man."

"I suppose you're right," he said with reluctance. "I reckon I must keep at it."

I knew I should say no more, but once again I couldn't help myself. He had to keep his attention focused on his work and not be distracted by temptation. He had to move on, to write about other topics beyond the Sternes. I knew I sounded like some sort of Puritan, but I couldn't bring myself to ignore his prior ill-judged involvements and wanton obsessions.

"It's so obvious, Billy," I said. "You've made great progress since distancing yourself from the Sternes. You should feel proud, and distance yourself even further."

Billy rolled his eyes. "You sound like Mr. Gilkes," he said. "What's more, your timing is wrong."

With a wry grin, he reached for a folded piece of yellow paper lying among the scribbled pages atop his cluttered desk. "Your advice, Doctor, though always well-intended, will be hard to follow. I received this telegram a couple of days ago— and after so many months without even a word."

He handed me the folded sheet. I opened it and read aloud: *"Please come to Marlow this Saturday afternoon. The staff and Mrs. Sterne will be absent. I owe you an apology."* It had been sent by Raphael Sterne.

"You see, Doctor," Billy said, lighting a cigarette, "he's been *incommunicado* for so long that I really can't turn the man down. His health is too fragile."

"Perhaps," I offered only half in jest, "he's figured out the identity of your 'literary fop.'"

Billy smiled and exhaled a small cloud of smoke. "Maybe he wants to pay me a compliment or two."

Billy's explanation seemed more farfetched than mine, and it pained me to think of his becoming involved with the Sternes again. But then I recalled Holmes' parting words about giving matters time to develop. I still didn't understand what Holmes meant, but I could see that he might actually appreciate hearing what was transpiring in Marlow. Against my better judgement, I said, "I'm sure Holmes and I would both appreciate a more recent account of the Sterne household."

But I had to add, "Although I can't for the life of me think why."

Billy rose from the bed to open the window. Despite the chill outside, the smoke from his cigarette was beginning to envelop us.

"Don't worry, Doctor," Billy said, exhaling into the night air. "You read the words. Mrs. Sterne won't even be there. You can rest easy; there should be no temptations. At least not of the human kind."

"One hopes not," I replied and stood up in preparation to leave. We shook hands. Considering my hostile reaction to so much of the first narrative he'd written, my final words to Billy before exiting could only be viewed as the greatest of ironies. "Don't forget to write a full report," I instructed. "I'll be sure to share it with Holmes."

Ω

Billy's second journal instalment follows:

Saturday morning
11 November 1911

Gentlemen:

Allow me some rambling thoughts as I journey back to Marlow:

My major hope is to—very quickly and without any serious complications—conduct my meeting with Sterne. It seems strange that on a Saturday the servants will be free and that Elaine will likewise be gone. Perhaps Sterne himself arranged it that way, so we can engage in private talks. From a purely selfish standpoint, I hold out hope that, since the last time I saw the man, his health has improved and his drinking is at last under some kind of control. However much I may detest Sterne's writing, I am continually trying to convince myself that today's visit might in some way be helpful in furthering my own career. I need more publications. If I intend to devote myself solely to writing, having my work printed only by The Academy *in London or* The Alleynian *at Dulwich is not going to produce the kind of money I need to live on. Whether or not I like his literary style, Raphael Sterne has the ability to promote my reputation. At the very least, he should be able to offer me some suggestions or opportunities.*

Ω

I have changed trains at Maidenhead. The closer I get to Marlow, the more optimistic I feel. I have convinced myself that Sterne's purpose in arranging this meeting is to repay me in some fashion. I helped settle him down. I secured his gun. He must finally have concluded that I am deserving of a reward. I'm sure that the apology he said he owes me in his invitation will take some sort of literary compensation.

Ω

I am now on the Marlow Donkey travelling into town, and I can honestly say that I'm looking forward to the visit. The grand blast of this little train's whistle underscores my optimism.

I plan to write the rest of my observations during my return trip to London . . . .

Ω

How mistaken can one be?

Despite the lateness in the year and coolness of the air, Sterne was sporting white duck trousers and a white shirt. He looked almost summery with his shock of black hair tumbling down his forehead.

As announced, the servants were gone, and so Sterne himself mixed just the one G-and-T for me, and I followed him up the stairs to the study that also served as his bedroom, the same room to which the butler and I had carried him after Elaine and I had found the poor devil bleeding in the garden. I eased into a soft chair while he chose the padded seat at his mahogany desk. The bullet hole in the ceiling above the bed still remained.

"You see?" he said, pulling out the top drawer. "No Webley."

I raised an eyebrow at the name.

"My pistol," he clarified, "a .455."

I smiled in mock recognition. (I will obviously need to learn about guns if I ever intend to incorporate them into my writing.)

"I've made a rather dramatic about-turn," he said. "The gun is gone. And I've been off alcohol for half a year now—ever since that terrible night in June."

"That terrible night in June" when we found him in the garden was really "that terrible night at the end of July," and

the actual date put it closer to four months instead of six, but I wasn't going to quibble. He sounded so proud of his accomplishments that it would have been churlish of me to contradict him. I'd come to regard him as tied to his liquor as closely as a dancehall girl to her red lipstick. Maybe that was why proclaiming his abstinence seemed his latest preoccupation.

His success doomed my hopes. The louder he shouted his freedom from alcohol, the more obvious became the true purpose of today's meeting—and it had nothing to do with my aspirations. I had been invited to Marlow to celebrate the triumph of Raphael Sterne. Despite the words in his telegram, there would be no offer of "apology" to me—let alone any hint of professional encouragement.

I blame myself, of course. I alone am responsible for my disappointment. I should have been more alert to the resurgence of egotism within the man; I had cautioned about it in my writing. Sterne had falsely convinced himself of his invulnerability before; to my deep consternation, he was in the process of doing so again.

"In fact," he boasted, "in honour of my noble self-restraint—as well as to commemorate your visit here in Marlow—I'm going to get myself a drink." He slapped his hand down on the closed desk top with a note of finality.

"Do you really think that wise?" I asked, standing up with the hope of keeping him seated.

He too rose. "Give me your glass," he insisted. "I shall return with more libations." He took my glass and marched down the stairs.

Alone, I had time to think. It was typical of the man's false modesty to proclaim his success in avoiding alcohol and then, as if it had been no great achievement, to undercut his accomplishment with a drink. Such reasoning gave me pause. If he backslid on the liquor, he might also backslide on the gun. I needed to be certain. No sooner did I hear the clink of glasses downstairs than I went over to the desk and opened the top drawer that he had shown me earlier. I had to be sure the gun was really gone. Though obviously no longer sticky, the dark drops of blood I'd seen before were still evident at the corner, but no weapon or ammunition remained in that drawer or in any of the others, all of which I carefully checked.

Just then I heard the man's footsteps on the stairs, and I retreated to my chair.

Sterne entered the room, offered me one of the G-and-T's he was carrying, and sat down.

"To temperance," he chortled, hoisting his glass.

"To irony," I replied.

On his second round, his memory seemed to engage. "Money," he said. "That's why I wanted you to come here. I've had a long time to think about it. You deserve some kind of remuneration for all the help you've given me."

Maybe I was wrong. Maybe he did have an apology planned all the while.

Sterne put down his drink, reached into his pocket, and produced a roll of currency.

"Nonsense," I replied. First, Leonard; now Sterne— everyone seemed to want to give me money. Although it looked quite tempting, I said, "Put your money away. I'm just a nurturing sort of bloke. I did what anyone else who was here

would have done." As I spoke the words, he replaced the bills in his pocket—rather too quickly, I judged. At the same time, I did wonder if anyone else besides me who'd been able to help Sterne that night in July would have followed his wife into her bedroom when the door swung open.

"You'll make some woman a devoted husband one day," he laughed. Then he ran his hand through his thick black hair. "Devoted," he repeated softly. A long moment later he murmured it once more while staring at his glass.

I said nothing. It wasn't my place to take his drink away.

"You'd reckon that a beautiful girl like Elaine would be enough for me." He took another pull of the gin. "What do you think?" he asked. "Isn't she beautiful?"

I began sweating as soon as he'd mentioned his wife. Once he posed these questions directly to me, I could feel my heart racing as well. Her body in the moonlight haunted my memory.

"Nothing to say on the subject?" he demanded, his mood turning sour. "Well, I'll answer the question myself. No, she is not enough for me! I've always had eyes for other women. Sylvia Leonard is a perfect example."

"The dead Sylvia Leonard? Lord Steynwood's daughter?"

Sterne leered. "Yes. The dead Sylvia Leonard. Lord Steynwood's daughter now deceased. The late wife of Terrence Leonard. I met her here in Marlow at a jumble sale. For charity. But I was just one of many. She had dozens of lovers, I can tell you."

He raised his glass once more. "To dead Sylvia." A short laugh escaped. "I'm the one who should be dead. I can't write anymore. Nothing comes to me. I've lost my touch."

So this was what became of writers who could no longer produce. They drowned themselves in alcohol and self-pity. I'd be sure to take note.

As the afternoon wore on, the room grew darker. Sterne was drinking straight gin now, and his eyelids were beginning to flutter. Finally, he gripped the arms of his chair, managed to rise to his feet, and stumbled backward onto his bed. He was out cold. It all felt rehearsed. I'd seen it before.

I tiptoed out of the room and down the stairs. I wanted to get back to London, but I didn't feel right about leaving Sterne alone in that condition. I'd witnessed once before what he was capable of doing to himself. I walked out to the garden and not far from the French windows sat down on a weathered, wooden bench amidst some purple foxgloves. I suppose I was waiting for anyone—the maid, the butler, the wife—to arrive at the cottage who could look out for the unconscious novelist, the same unconscious novelist who earlier I had been hoping would show me how to gain literary success. The more fool I.

Ω

Streaks of pale light still washed the sky awhile later when I got up to check on Sterne. He lay on his back exactly as he had when I'd left him earlier. Nothing in his room had been disturbed. I was beginning to get hungry; but instead of looking in the larder, I returned to Sterne's liquor cabinet and

174

fixed myself another drink. Only this time I found a bottle of Rose's Lime Juice and made myself a gimlet. Somehow it seemed fitting. When I returned to my bench by the foxgloves, I raised my glass. To Terrence Leonard, I said to myself, a victim once more. The scream of a train whistle answered my toast. It was probably the Marlow Donkey announcing its arrival.

Ω

I was now sitting in darkness. An hour passed. My Harris tweed kept the chill away, but there was no stopping the cold's ultimate embrace. A few more minutes crawled by, and another train whistle shrieked. I would finish my drink and head inside.

Before I could muster the energy to stand, I heard the distant ring of the front-door bell. Without the servants or the lady of the house available, I reckoned it was up to me to see who was there. I opened the door and found myself staring into the cornflower-blue eyes of Elaine Sterne.

"Oh," she said when she saw me. There was a note of disappointment in her voice. We hadn't separated on the best of terms back in July. "I forgot my key," she explained. "I thought Rafe would come to the door. I didn't expect you'd still be here."

"He invited me," I said. "I'm afraid he's been drinking again."

All she did was shake her head.

"He's knocked out upstairs in his bed, " I reported.

"I'll make some tea," she offered, slipping out of her long coat and placing it over the back of a nearby chair. She paused for a moment, as if to think, then added, "Why don't you go have a look at Rafe?"

I agreed and once again climbed the stairs.

Sterne's door was now closed. Maybe I was the one who'd shut it, but I didn't remember doing so. Maybe Sterne had got up to close it. I pushed it open and stared into darkness. I couldn't see anything, but a pungent smell overpowered all else. It was a sickly sweet smell that hadn't been there before. It was a smell you don't forget.

Never taking my eyes from where I knew Sterne to be lying, I ran my hand up and down the wall next to the doorjamb in search of the electric switch.

Immediately, the room was bathed in light, and I was confronted with death.

Raphael Sterne was lying on his left side, both feet still on the floor as if he'd been sitting at the edge of his bed and fallen over. His head extended over the side, and his right arm dangled towards the floor. His fingers remained inches away from an ever-increasing pool of red—its source, a trail of blood dripping down his face from a bullet hole in his right temple. His gun, the Webley, lay where he'd dropped it, in the centre of the ever-widening red pool. Sterne had obviously found some new place to stash the thing, a place where I couldn't find it—under a pillow, behind some books—it didn't really matter. No doubt he had expected that I'd search the desk to be sure the gun was really gone and that he could no longer be a danger to himself. I was wrong again.

My inaction surprised me, yet I knew I had to tell the dead man's wife. I left the light on and closed the door. Slowly, I walked down the stairs and into the sitting room where Elaine had set up for tea.

"And how is the melodramatic author today?" she asked.

At first I thought she meant me; then I remembered who the real author was.

"I think you should go up and have a look," I said cryptically. I knew it was wrong, that I should have prepared her for what she was about to see, that I should have told her that her husband was dead. But something perverse inside of me wanted her to feel the shock on her own. Maybe I wanted the impact of Sterne's death to cut through the wall of stoicism she seemed to be constructing. Maybe I was still angry with her and wanted her to feel the pain.

I heard her footsteps ascend the stairs, walk down the hallway, and enter Sterne's room.

Then I heard nothing.

A few moments passed before I headed up the stairway myself. Framed in the doorway, her back to me, Elaine was sobbing silently, her body quaking in response to the shock.

I approached her cautiously and dared to put an arm around her shoulder.

She shook me off.

I walked slowly down the stairs, out of the front door, and onto the pavement. On West Street I found a uniformed constable and told him what had occurred. He immediately sounded his whistle, reported the incident to the policeman who arrived in answer to the call, and then raced along with me back to the cottage while the second policeman ran off to the station. A local police motor-car arrived shortly thereafter.

Scotland Yard, I knew, would be round as soon as they possibly could.

Ω

It is now Sunday morning. With shaking hands and a half-closed eye, I force myself to write of one final event, which occurred last night and that I must include in this narrative.

After I had given my report to the police, Elaine insisted that I leave, and so I did. I still had time to make the final railway connections back to Paddington.

As I was returning to my room, a large, dark car—a Daimler, I think—rolled up to the kerb. A tall, thin old man with a white moustache got out. Dressed in evening suit and top hat, he was carrying a fashionable walking stick that had a silver handle. At first, I thought he might be some lost codger out for an evening on the town. The driver stayed inside, but another bloke—short, stocky, and much younger—followed the old man out of the car. I suddenly realized they were coming for me. It was fortunate that I had already folded and placed this narrative in my coat-pocket and out of harm's way, for in a moment the older man had pinned me against the wall of my building with his stick.

"Give up the Leonard case," he threatened.

"What?" I blurted out. I hadn't given Terrence Leonard a serious thought in months. If truth be told, when that motor-car arrived, I had been envisioning Elaine Sterne standing naked before me in her bedroom.

"Shall I instruct the bleeder, guv?" the shorter man asked.

The top hat nodded, and the right fist of the younger man pounded into my stomach. I doubled over, the wind knocked out of my gut, and then a knee caught me under the chin. I fell backward onto the cobblestones, and a quick kick struck my side.

"A boot to the chops, Guv?" I barely heard the younger man ask.

"Just the one," said the man with the stick.

He missed my jaw. A numbing blow to my temple was causing all to go black.

"That's for openers, sonny," I could just make out a disembodied voice growl. "Keep it up, and you might find yourself floating in the river."

"Yeh," the other man said, "pegged out."

I scarcely remember hearing them get back into the motor-car and rumble off down the road. But they must have. Somewhere I heard a violin playing Bach. And yet it still amazes me that, as I drifted into unconsciousness, I had the presence of mind to appreciate just how poetic the language of street-toughs can be . . . .

X

The moment a man sets his thoughts down on paper, however secretly, he is
in a sense writing for publication.
--Raymond Chandler
Working Notes

The news of Raphael Sterne's death brought Sherlock Holmes back to London the next day.

"I can't say that I'm surprised," he told me upon his arrival.

But at Sterne's inquest that Monday morning in Marlow, it was Billy who caused the sensation. Although Holmes and I had witnessed the damage to Billy's face the evening before, others simply stared, appalled to see Billy's bruises, the small cuts at his temple, his right eye swollen shut. His body too had suffered; for the first time his walking stick was more than a mere accessory. It had taken a Herculean effort to get himself out of bed the previous morning, write the final bit of his report, get cleaned up, and come to my house later in the day with his journal in hand, but he succeeded. I ministered to him, while Holmes read Billy's account of his latest trip to Marlow and the brutal beating that ended it. Once I'd finished attending to the young man's wounds, I too read the disturbing narrative.

It was obvious to Holmes and me that Billy had been attacked by Sebastian Moran and one of his minions. I wanted Youghal at the Yard to lock the blackguards up and throw away the key; but, as usual, Holmes' call for reason prevailed. One of Moran's many solicitors, he suggested, would argue that it was simply Billy's word against Moran's. Since Billy could produce no evidence that it was, in fact, Moran who'd conducted the attack, any such case against the villain would fall to pieces, and that would put an end to the matter. Billy was no physical fighter—certainly not against anyone as vicious as Sebastian Moran—but Billy trusted Holmes well enough to accept my friend's pledge. Holmes promised that, if there was any justice in the land, he would see to it that at the end of this affair Moran would have no further need for Billy.

The inquest itself was held in the large assembly room of Market House, Marlow's gloomy, old grey-stone town hall in the High Street. Although Mrs. Sterne formally identified her husband's body for the police, she did not attend the inquest. Since she was not the person who'd first discovered the body (that honour went to Billy) and since she said she was feeling too distressed to testify, the authorities did not require her presence. Not surprisingly, even without her observations on the deceased's deteriorating state of mind, the coroner concluded that the unfortunate victim, Raphael Sterne, had died by his own hand. Such an outcome seemed completely consistent with Billy's report to us.

And yet Sherlock Holmes appeared far from convinced. Beneath a threatening sky, Billy and I watched him silently prepare his briar, cross the street to the stone obelisk at the centre of the small ring road, and strike a match against its side.

"This won't do," he said mysteriously and exhaled a cloud of smoke that seemed to come from a fire within as much as from the tobacco in the bowl. "I had hoped that Youghal would be more discerning. He has a reputation for stirring the pot."

"It wouldn't be the first time Scotland Yard has bungled an investigation," I said, thinking of the clues missed at Lord Steynwood's town house in Mayfair. "And yet for the life of me, Holmes, I can't imagine what additional knowledge you have that the police do not."

Holmes smiled. "Why not share my knowledge with Mrs. Sterne?" he asked. "Perhaps her answers to the questions I pose will satisfy my concerns. I doubt it. But if you're up to it, Billy, we'll all three call on her, shall we? Trust me, gentlemen. There are much deeper goings-on here than this inquest has led us to believe."

Ever the gallant, Billy protested. "I'm not sure we should go see her, Mr. Holmes. Not because of my injuries— I'll make it, all right—but because she's so upset. She didn't even come to the inquest. Why would we want to distress her any further? Elaine deserves a time to rest."

"Elaine?" I repeated. Even if Billy sounded like Lancelot again, hoping to protect the Lily Maid of Astalot, his familiarity seemed completely misplaced regardless of past events.

Holmes let out another cloud of smoke, this one apparently borne of exasperation. "Perhaps, young man," he declared through gritted teeth, "a dose of reality will dampen your ardour." With great deliberateness, he added, "A female in repose is often a female in control."

Ω

Whatever Holmes' age, when he sensed the immediate resolution of a case, he could not be tethered; I, on the other hand, was feeling my years as well as my old war wound. On this occasion, he had to make allowances for Billy's limp; and so I managed to keep up with the two of them as they progressed along West Street. Billy had assured us that the Sternes' cottage was just minutes away, but with the town-hall clock in the cupola behind us striking noon and the ever darkening clouds promising rain, Holmes increased his gait, leaving Billy and me to scuttle along behind. Even more immediate to Holmes, I well knew, is that an unannounced arrival always puts the one to be questioned at a disadvantage.

The cantilevered house was every bit as unsettling as Billy had described it. With its steep roof, overhanging sections, and projecting windows, the cottage seemed the structural manifestation of the bizarre events that had occurred within. Only the black wreath at the entrance offered some sense of stasis. Holmes knocked on the door when suddenly rain exploded everywhere. We pulled our coats around us, but fortunately Mrs. Jenkins, the housekeeper, opened the door, and we followed her into the sitting room. A small fire glowed in the hearth, doing little to warm the room. A few moments later, heralded by a roll of thunder, Mrs. Sterne entered the scene. Dressed in black and standing tall, she looked like royalty in mourning.

"My God," she said upon seeing Billy's battered features. "What happened to you?"

"I'll be fine," he assured her. "Some people around here don't like me."

Mrs. Sterne placed a gentle hand against Billy's cheek. Her look of care and concern must have reflected all that Billy could ever have wished for. It seemed difficult for her to look away from him, but with some hesitation she finally addressed us all: "W-Welcome, gentlemen, although I-I can't begin to fathom what brings all three of you to see me."

"I believe condolences are in order," I offered.

"Yes," she said, clutching at the gold doubloon at her neck, "but the funeral isn't until tomorrow."

"Before then," Holmes said, "I have some questions I'd like to put to you, Mrs. Sterne."

"If you're up to it," Billy added reassuringly.

"I s-suppose so."

As we were seating ourselves, Mrs. Jenkins appeared. She desired to know if any sort of repast might be required; but with a quick shake of her head, Mrs. Sterne sent her away. An uncomfortable silence blanketed us, the staccato drumming of the rain the only distraction. Mrs. Sterne's gaze travelled from one of us to the other, no doubt seeking some form of comfort. She once again began twisting the intricate chain of her necklace.

"May I?" Holmes said, extending his left palm in her direction. "The doubloon, if you please."

Mrs. Sterne furrowed her brow. "I don't understand," she said.

"I would like to examine the engraving," Holmes replied. "It looks most interesting." He moved his left hand towards her again. He had seen the coin before, of course. But not until now had he studied its detail.

Reluctantly, Mrs. Sterne raised her hands to the back of her neck and, with arms up and elbows out, undid the clasp. A moment later, holding the golden coin in her left hand, she slowly poured the delicate chain on top of it with her right. Then she leaned forward and placed the collection in Holmes' extended palm.

Sherlock Holmes picked up the doubloon between the thumb and forefinger of his right hand, leaving the gold chain cupped in his left palm as if the delicate links had formed a tiny pool of water. Turning the coin so that the engraving faced outward, he held it up for Billy and me to inspect.

I leaned forward, but Billy, nodding in recognition, said simply. "I've seen it before; I thought it looked military."

In Billy's report, Holmes and I had both read of the engraving's design. Now we were seeing it close up for the first time. Facing outward, a small lion, adorned with a coronet, stood upon a large crown; the crown itself rested atop a rosette below which, in a flattened V shape, waved a blank banner.

"Quite military indeed," I echoed.

"Especially," Holmes added, "when you know the words that actually used to occupy that vacant banner. As, I'm sure, *you* do, Mrs. Sterne."

Elaine Sterne grew pale. "I-I don't know what you mean. I bought the piece at a jumble sale some time ago. I thought it had something to do with His Majesty."

"Is that what you told your husband?" Holmes asked.

"Why, yes, of course."

It was Billy who stated the obvious. "The blank banner—something must have been written inside."

My friend smiled. "Printed in English, the words, 'The Loyal Regiment.' Just as you observed, Billy—quite military, indeed."

"But the point, Mr. Holmes?" Billy asked.

"Mrs. Sterne?" Holmes prodded.

Elaine Sterne sat stone-faced, lacking the energy—or so it seemed—even to ask us to leave.

The little fire crackled feebly.

In the face of Mrs. Sterne's silence, Holmes supplied the explanation. "One day last July, when you, Watson, were attending your surgery, and when you, Billy, were coming out here to Marlow on your own, I took the opportunity to visit White Hall. I remembered enough about this engraving to reproduce it on paper; and since it is easily recognizable as a military insignia, I correctly assumed there was no better place to enquire about it than in the War Office."

"What did you learn?" Billy asked.

"One of the officers working there knew the design immediately. It is the badge of the Loyal North Lancashire Regiment. And they, gentlemen, as I'm certain Mrs. Sterne can confirm, served under Lieutenant-Colonel Robert Kekewich in the Boer War."

"Just a moment," I said. "Wasn't Kekewich the officer who commanded Terrence Leonard?"

"Yes, Doctor," Billy said, grimacing as he readjusted his position. "At Rooiwal."

"As you yourself reported to me a few months ago, Watson," Holmes added.

Throughout this seemingly digressive exchange, Mrs. Sterne was sitting perfectly still. She might almost have been holding her breath.

"And yet," Holmes continued, "at the War Office, when I examined the records of the Loyal North Lancashire during the Boer War, while I did discover some useful information, I could find no trace of Terrence Leonard."

"Some sort of error," I suggested.

"Perhaps."

"Mr. Holmes," Billy asked, "do you think that Terrence was lying to me about serving under Kekewich?"

"Before going to the War Office," my friend said, "I couldn't have provided a reliable answer to that question. But I did ask the officer I was speaking to if he knew of anyone who might have some specific knowledge of combat injuries suffered some thirteen or fourteen years ago. He directed me down a long corridor to the Office of Medical Records. At a small writing table within an office marked 'War Records' sat a clerk, pen in hand, noting figures in a ledger. As it turned out, he was compiling statistics on British military casualties suffered before 1900. Obviously, that included the Second Boer War, and after I'd introduced myself, he was quite helpful indeed."

"In what way?" Billy wanted to know.

"I asked him if he knew of the battle at Rooiwal. He had heard of it, he said; but, of course, he was just collecting numbers about those events. He couldn't recall the names from any records in particular, and he certainly couldn't account for a specific soldier's name not appearing on some list."

"Pity," I said.

"Yes," Holmes agreed, "but he did have a suggestion. He gave me the name of a surgeon in Harley Street, James Cuthbert, who, he told me, had actually served in South Africa and performed many a battle-related surgery."

"Cuthbert," I repeated. "I do believe I know the chap, Holmes. Tall, thin man with a narrow moustache. Friends with Dr. Doyle. They met in South Africa."

"Right you are, Watson."

"A bit on the sombre side, as I recall."

"Right again. But then who wouldn't be sombre after ministering to the horrific casualties that everyone fighting in South Africa would like to have forgotten? Or so I discovered after I'd left the War Office and gone to his surgery. He was good enough to make time in his schedule to hear me out."

"And what did you learn from him?" Billy asked.

If Mrs. Sterne had any interest in this medical tangent, she gave no indication. She continued to sit motionlessly, hands clasped tightly together, fingers entwined.

Holmes smiled. "It was clear that Dr. Cuthbert didn't know or recall the names of the men he had operated on all those years ago—at least, not at first. But once I described the white hair and the wounds to Terrence's face, the doctor began to remember."

"'Poor chap,' he observed through pressed lips that made him look all the more grim. 'Not often one gets half one's face blown away and lives. And all that white hair. Not common with young soldiers.' He stroked his moustache for a good minute or so, asking himself, 'What *was* his name?' He thought it might have started with an M; and with ever-gaining confidence, he tried out, 'Morrison? Marsten? Martin?' At this last attempt, his eyes lit up. 'Martin,' he announced. 'Yes, Martin. Paul Martin.'"

"No," Mrs. Sterne whispered. As silent as she had been during Holmes' account, we had paid her little mind. But now we could all see that, statue-like though she sat, tears were coursing down her cheeks.

Wincing in pain as he rose, Billy offered her his handkerchief. Catching her breath, she took the linen and daubed at her eyes. All of us turned to her questioningly. Who was this Paul Martin, and what was he to her?

"I loved him, you see?" she said in a voice we could hardly hear. "*Before* he was sent to the war. Terrence Leonard was Paul Martin then. We met in London, and he was the most beautiful lover I could ever hope to imagine. Handsome. Kind. Caring. For weeks, we spent every moment together. In a flat in Chelsea. Just before it was time for him to join his regiment, we married. And then he had to go. We pledged our love to each other, and I promised I would count the days until his safe return."

Married? To Paul Martin? Didn't that make Raphael Sterne her second *husband and Elaine Sterne a bigamist?*

Such complications didn't seem to matter to Billy. Still wincing, he sat at the edge of his seat, listening to her every word. I knew he was picturing himself in Terrence Leonard's shoes—if truth be told, in Terrence Leonard's bed with Terrence Leonard's wife—at least for those few weeks the young lovers had been together. Even I found myself envisioning how difficult it must have been to leave so gorgeous a creature as Elaine Sterne.

"But then," she continued, "I didn't hear from him, you see. I wrote many letters, but received no response. Months passed. Then a year. He was at war; I got no word. I presumed he was dead—wouldn't you?"

None of us dared to answer.

"Then I met Rafe, so charming and successful."

Billy's back stiffened at the mention of the writer.

"As far I knew," she continued, "Paul was gone. Why *shouldn't* I picture a beautiful new future with a distinguished man of letters? Who wouldn't have made such a choice? I believed my first husband to be dead, and so I married Rafe."

Mrs. Sterne paused to fold the linen she was holding.

"But then one evening," she said slowly, as if recalling a memory she must have examined over and over again, "Rafe and I were dining at the Savoy, and I saw Paul. My true husband. I was devastated."

She touched the handkerchief to her eyes again. "You all saw what he looked like when he returned. How horribly disfigured he was. The terrible scars. The snow-white hair. He was a different man. Yet I recognized his smile—crooked now, but warm nonetheless. He even had a different name. It was obvious that he didn't want me to see him this way. Obvious because he too had married again. But you all know this—that his wife was Sylvia Leonard, Lord Steynwood's daughter. She'd been a nurse during the war—that was how they'd met—she was used to that sort of thing, I suppose—the scars, the wounds, the blood. I was not."

Mrs. Sterne finished speaking and looked down at the handkerchief she was clutching. The silence that accompanied the end of her sad story allowed us to ponder the whirlwinds of emotion that were obviously raging within her breast.

It was Holmes who returned us to the world of practicality. "When did you have the doubloon made?" he asked.

"Just after Paul had gone to South Africa. I took a copy of one of his regimental badges to a jeweller who engraved the design on the coin. Except in place of the regiment's motto in the banner, I had him engrave our names. Once I'd met Rafe, I had them removed, of course. But I could never part with the coin itself."

"Why?" Billy persisted. "You'd given up on Terrence—or Paul. Why did you continue to wear the necklace?"

For the first time Mrs. Sterne managed a small smile. "A memory perhaps. A tribute to the evanescence of love."

As I looked into the glistening eyes of Elaine Sterne, I thought again of Tennyson's Elaine. This time I remembered how she had "lifted up her eyes and loved . . . with that love which was her doom."

Holmes was not so sentimental. "Maybe you wear the necklace to torture yourself for giving up on a man you thought you would be faithful to forever." He spoke in a most calculating tone. "Not to mention your foray into bigamy."

"Really, Holmes," I said, "you go too far. The woman has been through a terrible ordeal."

"No, old fellow" he replied, "we still have much farther to descend to get to the bottom of all this."

"All *what*?" Billy demanded of Holmes. "You've already pulled out from this poor woman the story of her two tragic marriages. We know Terrence killed Sylvia, and we know that Rafe killed himself. What more is there left to get to the bottom of?"

"I would like a sherry," Mrs. Sterne announced, a bizarre sort of answer to Billy's question.

"We might all do with one, " I suggested, "if it is not too great an imposition."

Mrs. Sterne rang for Mrs. Jenkins. A few moments later we were sitting with small cut-crystal glasses, each filled with the smoked-amber of Harvey's Bristol Cream.

"To lost love," Billy said, slowly raising his glass to Mrs. Sterne.

Ever the Lancelot, I thought as we three drank.

She bowed her head in reply. Then she too took a sip, and then another.

"And now, Mrs. Sterne," Sherlock Holmes said in his most serious tone, "pray tell us what really happened to Terrence Leonard's second wife."

Billy's eyes widened at the question; Mrs. Sterne, returning her glass to the table, seemed prepared to fulfil Holmes' request.

"I don't know where Rafe met that whore," she said angrily. "And I don't care. I don't know where he found so many of the tarts he took up with. He spent lots of time with Sylvia, but when I discovered that she—not to mention Paul— was our neighbour in Marlow, I for one refused to be fooled. I told Rafe to leave her alone—I pleaded with him. At first, he just laughed. But I wouldn't give up, and he finally seemed to come round. He said he would break it off with her; and to be certain he did, I followed him to her London house the next night all the way from Marlow. I stood by an open French window outside the drawing room, and I heard Rafe tell her he was done with her. But she said she'd never let him go. He pleaded with her, but she just laughed. And so Rafe picked up a small statue and beat her head in with it."

Mrs. Sterne covered her eyes with her hands, as if she could blot out the horrible scene she had witnessed.

"No wonder Sterne had been drinking so much," Billy said. "After what he'd done. No wonder he sought out a place like Dr. Vering's."

"Small wonder," I observed, "that he ultimately took his own life."

"And yet," Billy charged Mrs. Sterne, "you allowed Terrence to take the blame for your husband's crime. The man you once loved, or said you did. He confessed falsely. My God, he killed himself. All because he loved you."

Billy forced himself to lean back in his chair. He seemed to be putting distance between himself and the lady.

For her part, Mrs. Sterne began sobbing quietly. It was as if she had recognized the desertion of her most gallant supporter.

Sherlock Holmes put his fingers together in that familiar steeple; if we hadn't been listening to so melancholy a tale, I might almost have thought he looked amused.

"What next, Mrs. Sterne?" he prodded. "Do tell."

"I had to protect my husband. I got Rafe to change his bloody clothes and boots—he had some clothing left in that woman's London house. I found a Gladstone bag in a closet, and I stuffed Rafe's things into it along with the statue he'd used to hit her with. We took a cab to Paddington and made our way back here to Marlow. Once we got off the train, I put him into a hansom and sent him home. Then, so he wouldn't be linked to his crime, I carried the Gladstone from the railway stop to the Thames and threw it off the bridge into the river. I stood there for a few minutes watching the evidence that could incriminate my husband sink slowly into the water."

"My God," Billy whispered again.

"A Gladstone full of clothes, heavy shoes and a bronze statue," Holmes observed dubiously. "It must have weighed a lot. How did you manage to carry it on your own all the way down to the river?"

"A crisis makes a woman strong, Mr. Holmes," she said.

"Strong enough to throw it over that high wooden fencing on the end of the bridge nearest to the railway station?" Holmes asked.

"Yes," she said. "Even so."

"But, Mrs. Sterne," Holmes announced with great deliberation, "here in Marlow, there is no high wooden railing near the station." He paused to let the implication resonate.

Her unmarked brow began to furrow.

"You never threw them anywhere, did you?" Holmes charged.

Mrs. Sterne sucked in her breath and then exploded into tears.

Not even Billy came to her rescue this time.

"And so, Mrs. Sterne," Holmes said, "we have come to the crux of the problem: who was it who really killed Sylvia Leonard?"

Billy and I sat speechless, spellbound by the drama unfolding before us.

"It was you who murdered Sylvia Leonard," Holmes persisted, "was it not?"

At first, she said nothing. She merely sat there, taking it all in. Then she slowly nodded. "That whore told Rafe she'd never let him go," Mrs. Sterne said, her voice a near whisper. "So I shot her."

Holmes reached into his coat pocket and produced a small paper envelope, the same envelope he had used to collect clues at the scene of Sylvia Leonard's murder. He displayed for all of us to see the pale strand of hair he'd extricated from the light-blue carpet near the bloodstains. I should have remembered the old rule: one sees what one expects to see. I had originally thought the strand to be white, evidence from the head of Terrence Leonard; I could see now that it was not white, but blond.

Pinching the single golden hair between his right thumb and index finger, he held up the strand next to Mrs. Sterne's shining locks. "Behold the incriminating evidence," Holmes announced.

"But the beating?" Billy asked. "Certainly, Elaine—Mrs. Sterne—couldn't have accomplished that."

"No," said Holmes, "she did not. Strange as it may seem, with all of his antics, Raphael Sterne still did love his wife. So much so that when he watched her shoot his mistress—after Mrs. Sterne had followed him and confronted the woman—it was he who beat in Sylvia Leonard's head. He was attempting to cover up the wound caused by the bullet from the Webley that might have led the police to his wife—

the same bullet that had passed through Sylvia's head and lodged in the wall, the same bullet that produced the bullet hole which Scotland Yard has yet to discover."

Billy now sat upright in his chair, narrowing his eyes and nervously flexing his right foot. It was clear that he was absorbing all that he'd heard, trying to make some sense of it, trying to comprehend these depraved facets of human behaviour that he was obviously encountering for the first time in reality.

"So," Billy said to Elaine Sterne, "Rafe, your second husband, killed himself to assure that the murder which *you* had committed would be blamed on *him*—just as Terrence had done before." The deliberateness in his voice suggested the deliberations in his brain; he might have been trying out some devious plot line in some macabre work of fiction.

"Oh, Ray," she said, never calling him Billy as Holmes and I always did. "I killed Rafe too. I slipped into the house that day while you were in the garden, and I shot him when I knew the Marlow Donkey would sound its whistle and cover the sound. I only pretended not to have a key when you let me in."

Billy's mouth dropped open. He too had been a victim. Raising his eyebrows, he looked as if he was going to ask a question. But he never did.

"Once Rafe stopped drinking," she continued, "the more rational he was becoming, and the more he started talking to me about what I had done to Sylvia. I couldn't take the chance that one day he might tell the truth. That's why I kept his soiled clothes. So I could use them to implicate him if I ever needed to. I couldn't give him that much power over me.

I had to remain in control. That's why I originally came to you, Mr. Holmes—to get *you* *to* find Rafe. When I went to Scotland Yard to report Rafe's disappearance, I overheard Inspector Youghal say that Sherlock Holmes was investigating Sylvia Leonard's death. That's the real reason I chose you to find my missing husband."

And so the story was complete, Holmes' reputation as a master crime-solver the ironic hook that had brought Elaine Sterne to my premises in the first place.

Like an ice princess, Mrs. Sterne now rose; as a consequence, so did we all.

"And now," she said, hands clasped in front of her, "I must ask you gentlemen to be so kind as to leave. I am quite exhausted. I shall expect the police in the morning." With that, she mustered whatever pride she had left and withdrew from the room, leaving us to find our own way out.

Ω

It was late afternoon when the three of us approached the tiny railway station in Marlow. The rain had stopped, and long shadows wrestled with reflections of fading sunlight on the wet ground. From a telegraph office in West Street, we had already notified Scotland Yard of Mrs. Sterne's confession. But once informed, Youghal apparently doubted our claims; though he did order a local constable to remain standing in front of the cottage, Youghal himself had no plans to come all the way out to Marlow to see Mrs. Sterne until the following day. His recalcitrance surprised none of us.

We were but a few paces from the station when suddenly, highlighted by final vestiges of the setting sun, the low white suspension bridge that crossed the Thames came into view.

"Holmes," I asked, pointing in its direction, "you've never been down there by the water. How did you know there was no high wooden railing where Mrs. Sterne said she'd thrown the bag?"

"I hadn't the foggiest clue, old fellow," he said. "But the more important fact is that neither did she."

XI

If you press exactly the right buttons and are also lucky, justice may show up in the answer.
--Raymond Chandler
The Long Goodbye

The weather turned even colder the next day; but when Inspector Youghal arrived at Queen Anne Street just after lunch, his furrowed brow signalled more than just the bad weather. We met him in the sitting room, and he offered a grim nod. I indicated a chair, but he refused, and we all remained standing.

"I owe you an apology, Mr. Holmes," he began. "I should have got out to Marlow immediately."

Holmes and I exchanged concerned glances as Youghal reached inside his coat pocket and produced a photographic copy of a handwritten note.

"Gentlemen," the inspector announced in his most official tone, "you should know that Mrs. Elaine Sterne committed suicide last night. I thought you should be informed. She took arsenic—her husband had it in the house, something related to his book-writing and the study of poisons. The housekeeper, Mrs. Jenkins, found her dead this morning in bed with this note lying beside her. The original, as you can see, was written on fine stationery."

Holmes then read aloud: *"It's all over now. I shot and killed Sylvia Leonard, watched my husband Raphael Sterne try to help me by obliterating the bullet wound, and I let my legal husband Paul Martin, later known as Terrence Leonard, take the blame. Because of my silence, Paul killed himself. For my own protection, I shot and killed Rafe.*

"Three people (four, counting myself) are dead because of me. I wish I had never been born. The only person who stands out in this sordid tale is the young writer people call Billy but I know as Ray. Throughout the ordeal, he maintained his loyalty to the man he knew as Terrence Leonard. I can only pray that I was somehow deserving of some minute share of the attention he showered on me.

"It is signed, *Elaine Sterne*."

"My word," was all I could think of saying.

"Needless to say," Youghal added, 'Raphael Sterne's funeral scheduled for today has been put off."

Holmes offered the note back to the inspector, but Youghal shook his head.

"You keep it," he said. "Lord Steynwood doesn't want this letter made public. Hopes to avert a scandal. Wants to let Terrence Leonard—that is, Paul Martin—remain the culprit despite the fact that we now know he was innocent."

"If I may, Inspector," I asked, "if Lord Steynwood wants it kept quiet, why risk additional people learning what really happened by making a copy—"

"Multiple copies, actually," he corrected.

"—Multiple copies then. Aren't you tempting fate?"

The policeman laid a finger against the side of his nose. "Let's just say, Doctor, that simply because a rich bloke like His Lordship wants something done a certain way, don't mean that's the way it's going to get done—if you take my point. Even us lads at Scotland Yard believe in justice."

Holmes and I both responded with appreciative smiles. After all, the more copies there were, the more difficult it would be to identify whoever was responsible for making any one or all of them public.

"Besides," Youghal added, "I'm simply sharing evidence with trusted colleagues. It's part of my job."

"Speaking of evidence," Holmes said, "any sign at the Sterne house of a Gladstone filled with bloody clothes, a pair of boots, and an antique statue?"

Youghal's eyebrows shot up in surprise. "Blimey, Mr. Holmes! You astound me. You really do. My men did find such a bag covered with *débris* and tools at the rear of the potting shed. It contained precisely the contents you mentioned."

"So *that* part of her story was true, eh, Holmes?"

"Yes, Watson. It was just as she said: she didn't throw the bag into the river at the end; she kept it close at hand should she ever have needed to implicate Sterne even more."

I thought of Billy; he deserved to hear the sordid *dénouement* of this already sordid tragedy. "Might we show it to—"

Reading my mind, Holmes cut me off. "Thank you, Inspector," he said, shaking the policeman's hand.

No sooner had Youghal taken his leave than I proposed sending a telegram to Billy asking him to come round.

"Tell him to meet us at the Crown and Eagle," Holmes said. "Somehow, that establishment seems the appropriate place to lay this case to rest once and for all."

Ω

In retrospect, it really wasn't as great a coincidence as it had seemed. But arriving at the Crown and Eagle a short time before our appointed meeting with Billy late in the afternoon, we couldn't help noticing a familiar black Daimler parked at the kerb nearby. Thus it was with caution that we entered the taproom and a greater sense of alertness once we saw the profile of Colonel Sebastian Moran.

Seated at a far table and facing a stranger, Moran was easy enough to identify. One couldn't miss his drooping moustache, high forehead, thin strands of white hair curling over the collar of his black coat, and that insidious cane lying within reach on the wooden chair next to him. On this occasion, he appeared in so intimate a conversation that he didn't notice Holmes and me arrive. In his younger years, he would have been more alert to our presence.

It was the other man, literally cloaked in mystery, that we failed to recognize. Not only did he wear a long, heavy coat that blanketed his body, but a grey woollen stocking cap pulled down to his eyes and covering much of the stringy red locks that fell to his shoulders, a full ginger beard that hid his lower face, and a black woollen scarf that encircled his chin and neck. Yet despite all this concealment, there was something familiar about him, which I couldn't place.

Holmes and I quietly collected our pints at the bar; and Holmes, motioning towards a small table near the door, led us to our seats. Such a vantage point prevented our having to march across the floor directly into Moran's line of vision. After huddling behind our tankards, Holmes indicated with his head the two men we were watching. "Watson," he whispered, "observe what the stranger is drinking."

Moran was sampling a sherry. But the liquid in his companion's glass bore the unmistakable yellow-greenish tinge of Rose's Lime Juice. Based on our previous experience in this very pub, if I had to guess, I would identify the potation in question as a gin gimlet.

Suddenly I re-examined the stranger, erasing in my mind the hat, the hair, the beard. Even though the scarf and beard covered the scars, I now could make out the half-closed left eye.

"My God, Holmes," I said softly, "it's Terrence Leonard."

Holmes nodded. "I thought as much, Watson, but remember that I've never seen him. I needed your corroboration." With that, he put his hand into his pocket and pulled something out.

Just then the two men completed their conversation and stood up. It was startling to see Sebastian Moran embrace anyone, but that is exactly what he did. It was but a moment later, as he was tossing some coins onto the table to pay for the drinks, that he saw Holmes and me.

Terrence Leonard pretended to ignore us as he made his way towards the exit just beyond our table. In leaving, he had to pass close by; and when he did so, Holmes passed whatever he was holding into Leonard's palm. Then the ghost was gone.

For his part, stick in hand, Moran strode right up to us. "Holmes," he declared, "I won't say that all is forgiven between us because it is not. But you deserve some credit for setting the record straight. Terrence Leonard, a true British hero of Rooiwal, was no murderer. I was in that war, as you know; and a soldier with his courage deserved much better than what some threw at him here in England."

"You speak of him in the past tense," I offered, thinking of the man with whom we'd just seen Moran conversing. "Surely—"

"Enough, Dr. Watson," he snarled. "I've said too much already."

"However oblique your compliment about setting the record straight," Holmes said to Moran, "it is accepted."

Moran began to turn, but Holmes blocked his way. "One more thing, Moran. Now that all this business is cleared up, I want to assure our young friend that you have no more interest in him."

Moran smiled. "You can tell that bloody fool that he has nothing more to fear from Colonel Sebastian Moran. Would that I could say the same for you, Sherlock Holmes."

With that, the villain whirled and marched out through the doorway, almost knocking over Billy who, at that dramatic moment, was just making his entrance into the pub.

Ω

Billy stood frozen, his back pinned against the open door. In amazement, he watched stalk by him the man who'd been responsible for delivering the bruises Billy still was wearing. Then Billy looked in our direction. Holmes, who'd been drumming a nervous finger on the table, motioned him over. "We have news for you," he said to the lad, "and I'm not certain how you'll take it."

Billy looked quizzically at my friend and then gently eased his body into the empty chair next to Holmes. "About Moran?" he asked, trying to anticipate what he was about to hear. "That was him I just saw, wasn't it?"

"Yes," Holmes said. "You did just see Moran. But the news I have is about Terrence Leonard."

Billy's eyes narrowed.

"Terrence Leonard's not dead," Holmes announced softly. "In fact, not more than five minutes ago, we saw him right here in the Crown and Eagle. Watson identified him."

Billy said nothing. A furrow lined his brow as he absorbed the information. "You're certain, are you?" he asked at last.

"Yes," Holmes said.

"Bloody Hell!" he exploded. "Why would he have pretended suicide then?"

Holmes shrugged. "Probably because Lord Steynwood wanted to keep him dead. That way, the story about Lord Steynwood's murdered daughter would remain dead as well— Inspector Youghal's hopes notwithstanding. Maybe His Lordship paid Terrence off; maybe he'd paid Terrence from the start to take the blame."

"But where's Terrence staying? Where does he live?" Billy began to rise as if to go out and look that very moment for his resurrected friend.

I laid a hand on the young man's arm, and he sat down again.

"Billy," Holmes cautioned, "think about it. Terrence Leonard wants to stay hidden. He's changed his appearance as much as he can. He just walked past Dr. Watson without a nod. If he changes his mind, he knows where all of us live and could find us if he wanted. But he obviously does *not* want to. Leave him be."

"Terrence alive?" Billy muttered more to himself than to Holmes or me. A bit wobbly, he stood up and made for the bar. "I need a drink," he said to us over his shoulder.

Billy returned with a gin gimlet, and Holmes explained to both of us what he'd deduced months earlier in connection with his visit to the War Office. "Moran helped Leonard counterfeit the suicide. When that dynamite blew up in Terrence's face, it turned out that one of the men he'd saved was a soldier named Enoch Parker. Enoch Parker, it turns out, works for Moran. In point of fact, Enoch's the son of Parker the garrotter, the killer who stood sentinel for Moran when the colonel tried to shoot my wax figure from the empty house in Baker Street. Enoch is actually Moran's godson. In fact, you yourselves have seen them both together."

"We have?" Billy and I cried simultaneously.

"Enoch's Moran's driver," Holmes explained. "In the Daimler. The young man with the aquiline nose. Enoch Parker is chauffeur for his own godfather."

"But-but," I sputtered, "how did you know that this-- this Enoch Parker—had been at Rooiwal?"

"When I unsuccessfully searched the records for Leonard's name under Kekewich's command at Rooiwal, I did come across young Parker's. I remembered that the elder Parker had a close connection with Moran and that Moran, like Enoch, was off fighting the Boers. With the help of the police, it wasn't difficult to determine that Enoch was the son of Parker the garrotter."

"Good work, Holmes," I said.

"Once it was obvious to me that Terrence didn't kill anyone, I assumed that his suicide must have been staged. And who better equipped with nefarious contacts to make it all seem real? I'm certain that Moran provided the boat, the writing paper, the stones, the transportation from Loch Ness, and even the rather elaborate disguise we were subjected to today. Out of gratitude for saving his godson's life, Colonel Moran proved quite the help to Terrence Leonard."

"The Tankerville Club!" I suddenly remembered. "Where Terrence had worked. I *knew* there was some link to Moran."

Holmes looked quizzical. Yet I was certain that he too would recall the gambling scandal he had once helped resolve in that unsavoury place.

"Billy told me," I explained to Holmes, "that Terrence had been working at the Tankerville while he was trying to change the course of his life."

"Yes," Billy said, "that's true."

"Billy," I said, "do you recall that there was something about the club that I couldn't bring to mind? I realize now what I'd forgotten: Moran himself was a member!"

Sherlock Holmes didn't register surprise often. On this occasion, his eyebrows rose just enough to show concern. "What you *also* seem to have forgotten, Watson," he said, "was to furnish *me* with that information. Obviously, Moran secured a position there for Leonard. Moran had been an even greater help to Leonard than I realized. Now if I had learned of that link between Leonard and Moran when *you* did, Watson . . . ." He didn't complete the sentence; he didn't need to.

"What a coincidence that you ran into them here," Billy said, rescuing me from my embarrassment.

"Yes and no," Holmes replied. "Moran might have been able to get Leonard employment and even change his appearance, but he couldn't transform Terrence Leonard's taste in liquor or the surroundings he wanted to taste it in. So encountering Moran and Leonard in this particular establishment was not so fortuitous after all. On the other hand, our being here at the precise moment they were is what I believe they call in your homeland 'a lucky break'."

Billy blushed at Holmes' reference to America.

"What's more," I said, "Moran told us that you have nothing more to fear from him."

Billy raised his glass. "Just as you promised, Mr. Holmes," he said and drank some gin.

Holmes nodded in appreciation. But he knew as well as I that it was now time for the most difficult task, the reason we had summoned Billy to the Crown and Eagle in the first place.

"I'm afraid we have some other news for you, lad," I said, placing my hand on top of his. "Sad news," I added, hoping to soften the blow.

Holmes presented to the young man the copy of Mrs. Sterne's suicide note.

Billy read it calmly enough. Or so it appeared. When he was done, he ran his hand across the table to be sure the wood was dry, laid the paper on it, and stared into his gimlet for a moment. Then he took a long pull, put the glass down, and gazed at the note.

Suddenly, as if struck by divine revelation, he announced, "I'm going to publish this letter! In an article for *The Academy.* I'm going to explain it all. I'm going to depict the rot and corruption that led all these people to do what they did, and I'm going to reveal Lord Steynwood as the duplicitous, conniving cockroach that he is."

Ordinarily, I might have tried to stop Billy. But remembering Youghal's incriminating portrait of His Lordship, as well as the policeman's desire for exposing the story, I kept my thoughts in reserve. I do recall thinking that Dulwich's Headmaster, Mr. Gilkes, would be proud of Billy's hunger for justice.

Holmes said this: "Be careful, Billy. Lucius Ward did not become Lord Steynwood by countenancing dissenters. Many a career has been dashed on the rocks of righteousness—despite the virtue of the cause."

Billy stared grimly at my friend. "While I fancy myself an Englishman, Mr. Holmes," the young man said, "I cannot forget, as you just reminded me, that I was born in America. And the bells of freedom and justice ring as loudly in my head here in England as they would if I were back in the States."

"Even at the expense of your writing career?" I asked.

Billy contemplated my question. "Elaine died to clear the names of Terrence and her husband," he said. "Terrence destroyed his own life to protect hers. Out of respect to all three of them, I must expose the Truth."

At the end of this noble statement, he tossed down the remainder of his drink, pushed his chair from the table, and stood up. He reached for the suicide confession, and after carefully placing it in a breast pocket, strode out into the darkness.

Ever the knight errant, I remember thinking as a cold wind blew into the pub through the door Billy had opened. Moments later, Holmes and I exited as well.

"One last point I need clarified," I said to Holmes as we made our way down Southampton Row.

Holmes smiled, as if anticipating my question.

"Back there in the Crown and Eagle," I said, "when Terrence Leonard walked past us as he was leaving, what did you hand to him?"

"Mrs. Sterne's doubloon," he said. "I cadged it in Marlow. I thought he should have it. It seems only fitting."

XII

To say good-bye is to die a little.
--Raymond Chandler
The Long Goodbye

Not that one can ever speak of the Christmas holiday as routine, but in truth it was in late December of 1911 that familiar habits began to reassert themselves in Queen Anne Street. Earlier in the month Mrs. Watson returned from her sojourn in the country and between her and Mrs. Meeks, the rhythm of the household was re-establishing itself. The house was swept, the tree was ornamented, the goose was purchased. In the spirit of the season, my wife even suggested we invite Sherlock Holmes to join us for Yuletide merriment. Yet in his most proprietary fashion, Holmes declined the offer. Due to the Leonard case, he wrote, on too many occasions during the last few months he'd been forced to leave his bees in the care of someone else. We were not to worry about him missing out on warm Christmas cheer, he cautioned, because he was certain that Mrs. Hudson would concoct just the right hot toddy for celebrating the holiday on a cold winter's night.

As for Billy, we heard nothing of the lad from the moment he'd marched out of the Crown and Eagle. Although it seemed clear that his intention was to return to his digs and compose some fearsome diatribe against Lord Steynwood, the news of the murders continued to lie dormant. Whatever

Billy's intentions, Holmes and I had agreed not to disseminate the facts surrounding the deaths of Raphael Sterne and his wife; and for all of Inspector Youghal's prodding, his attempts seemed to have had no effect whatsoever. Let Billy, prompted by his own inner turmoil, disclose what he felt compelled to reveal. Whatever positive might come from the tragic events, the responsibility would be Billy's. If anyone had a way of fashioning a story of murder and suicide into some sort of exemplum, the passionate young man from Dulwich College, with the moral teachings of Mr. Gilkes and his own strong literary opinions to guide him, seemed just the writer to do so.

With the familiar melodies of holiday carols still ringing in my ears and the violent strains of our recent mystery ebbing from my mind, I began 1912 with little thought of the Sternes, the Leonards, or Lord Steynwood. The New Year had already advanced two days, and there was no cause to make any connection between the harrowing events of the previous months and the stranger who approached my surgery in the early afternoon. The young gentleman in high collar and frock coat arrived just as I was preparing to leave.

"Dr. Watson," he asked, consulting a small sheet of notepaper. "Dr. John H. Watson?"

"Yes, I am Dr. Watson. But, as you can see, my surgery is now closed for the day."

He extended a soft hand. "My name is Denis Woodbury, sir. I'm not here as a patient. I am, in fact, secretary to Mr. Cecil Cowper, editor of *The Academy and Literature Magazine*."

"*The Academy and Literature Magazine?*" I repeated. It took me a moment, but then I recognized the full title of the journal for which Billy had been writing. "Ah, yes, *The Academy*!"

"Quite correct, sir," Mr. Woodbury said stiffly. "If I might get right to the heart of the matter, sir, Mr. R.T. Chandler, whom I believe you know, has been contributing to our publication for more than a year now."

I nodded, still mystified by what any of this had to do with me.

"It appears that Mr. Chandler has listed yourself, Doctor—along with a Mr. Sherlock Holmes, whom Mr. Chandler identifies as a 'consulting detective, retired'—as references to his good character. Since Mr. Holmes seems to live in Sussex and you, of course, are right here in London, Mr. Cowper has asked me to have a friendly word with you regarding Mr. Chandler's recent work."

Not having heard from Billy in months, I was more than a bit surprised to be contacted on his behalf. Nevertheless, I ushered Mr. Woodbury into my consulting room. I took the wooden chair at my desk, and he, the one opposite, the seat generally occupied by my patients.

"Now, sir, what can I do for you?" I asked.

Mr. Woodbury cleared his throat. "To be perfectly frank, Dr. Watson, Mr. Cowper is greatly concerned with what he calls an 'obsession' on the part of Mr. Chandler."

Recalling our last exchange with Billy, I could easily imagine where this conversation was leading, but I dutifully asked my guest to explain the nature of this alleged affliction.

"Mr. Chandler persists in writing some sort of denunciation of Lord Steynwood," Mr. Woodbury announced. "Some humbug about concealing evidence that reveals the true nature of a number of untimely deaths. Mr. Cowper has encouraged Mr. Chandler to return to the more usual topics he has sent to us. Mr. Cowper has appreciated Mr. Chandler's essays like "The Genteel Artist" and "The Remarkable Hero"—attacks, as it were, on what Mr. Chandler calls the 'preciousness' in literature. Such articles contain the kind of literary analysis that our readers have come to expect from—if I may say—so insightful a periodical as *The Academy*. In actuality, just this week we are publishing Mr. Chandler's most recent submission. It is entitled 'Realism and Fairyland', and it extols the virtues of idealists who can create beauty out of dust. Mr. Cowper lays proud claim to having printed numerous noteworthy compositions by Mr. Chandler. But, to be perfectly frank, Dr. Watson, crime thrillers, whether real or fictive, have no place in our magazine—regardless of their source."

"And how did Mr. Chandler react to your objections?" I asked.

Here Mr. Woodbury cleared his throat again. "He defends himself by saying that one of the deaths in question is that of Raphael Sterne, the noted novelist. Mr. Chandler argues that Sterne's importance in the world of *belle-lettres* should render unnecessary any question of relevance regarding the piece."

Although I recognized the disingenuousness in Billy's explanation, I added my support and that of Holmes *in absentia*. "It's only fair to tell you, Mr. Woodbury, that both Sherlock Holmes—who is indeed a consulting detective, the world's first—and myself, his colleague, have also been involved in solving this very real puzzle that Mr. Chandler has referred to."

Mr. Woodbury raised a single eyebrow in apparent disapproval.

"Does not Mr. Cowper," I asked, "find merit in the argument that this matter has significant literary relevance?"

"Absolutely not. In the first place, as I would have thought Mr. Chandler also believed, the lurid work of the late Mr. Sterne is not the kind of high-minded prose we like to promote in our magazine. In the second place, if I may be perfectly frank," and here, leaning forward, Mr. Woodbury spoke *sotto voce,* "regardless of Mr. Cowper's personal feelings, it has been made known to us in the publishing industry—an industry that, although widely scattered, is still a part of Lord Steynwood's vast dominion—that His Lordship forbids any publication whatsoever of Mr. Chandler's composition by magazine, newspaper, or book. The appearance of this piece—or even a reference to it—will result in the immediate termination of the publishing house that is responsible—no matter how successful, important, or popular."

Mr. Woodbury took a white linen handkerchief from an inner breast pocket and pressed it against his forehead. Despite the coolness of the January air, he was perspiring freely. "Lord Steynwood is a most influential figure," he proclaimed. "When His Lordship speaks, all Fleet Street listens. And to be perfectly frank, Dr. Watson, I need not remind you that Lord Steynwood has the power to carry out his threat."

No, to be perfectly frank, Mr. Woodbury did not need to remind me.

"I'm not certain how familiar you are with *The Academy*," the secretary continued, "but since its merger with *Literature* magazine about ten years ago, it has undergone a number of changes in ownership and, therefore, changes in editorial philosophy. Thanks to the notoriety that accompanied the controversial friendship between its previous editor, Lord Alfred Douglas, and the writer, Oscar Wilde, the publication can now ill afford any kind of dispute with the so-called 'czar of the printed word.' In short, Mr. Chandler has been instructed to cease promoting this notorious piece of his or, to be perfectly frank, his employment will be terminated. His contract rescinded."

"And his response?"

"He resigned."

Left of his own volition—that sounded like our Billy.

"But if he has resigned, Mr. Woodbury, why have you come to see *me*? Are you not finished with him then?"

"Mr. Cowper sees promise in the man. That's why he wanted me to encourage *you* to speak to Mr. Chandler. Mr. Cowper was hoping that *you* could talk some sense into Mr. Chandler in order to save the man's writing career. For rest assured, Dr. Watson, that if Mr. Chandler persists in demanding to make public this murder story of his, he will have no literary future in England."

"Ah," I sighed. "But, you see, Mr. Chandler claims that his independent streak comes from across the ocean. He was born in America, after all. Chicago, to be exact."

Mr. Woodbury's eyes widened. "No, I didn't know." He daubed at his brow again, as if preparing himself for a final thrust. "Well, Dr. Watson," he said, "if Mr. Chandler hopes to become a successful writer and if Mr. Chandler was indeed born in America as you say, then perhaps—to be perfectly frank—he ought to consider going back."

Message delivered, Mr. Woodbury returned his linen to his inner breast pocket and appeared ready to rise. Yet he did find it necessary to make one last point. "You know, Doctor, Lord Steynwood's hand is far-reaching. And while I possess but a limited familiarity with the publishing industry, I do feel confident in predicting that Mr. Chandler's narrative will never see the light of day—even if he *does* return to America. Between us, Doctor, I've heard it said that Lord Steynwood will be certain that no hint at all of Chandler's connection to the Sterne case will ever be published. Anywhere."

His final arrow seemed aimed at me. "For that matter, Dr. Watson, I would also be surprised if any reference about a connection between Raymond Chandler and you and this Mr. Sherlock Holmes ever appears in print."

With these last words left to reverberate in my head, Mr. Woodbury stood up, nodded in my direction, and exited.

I watched him close the door. When he was out of earshot, I called after him, "And a Happy New Year to you too, sir." Then I locked the surgery and, having lost interest in my usual luncheon and nap, shuffled aimlessly into the house.

Ω

In late April of 1912, news of the *Titanic*'s sinking a few weeks before still dominated the newspapers, usurping much talk about anything else. Some observers were predicting that a hundred years later people would still be fascinated by the arrogance and madness that led to the demise of so many unfortunates, both rich and poor.

Despite the power of the tragedy at sea (not to mention the weeks Holmes and I had spent working together on other matters), it was our young friend Billy the page who once again came to occupy our thoughts. He had written to me that he wanted to leave England and return to the United States. At first glance, it might appear that he was following the advice of Denis Woodbury; but in point of fact, just as Woodbury had predicted, Billy was having great difficulty ridding himself of the acrid bitterness, sour disappointment, and burning rage that had so recently been plaguing his writing career.

At the same time, the resentment in his Uncle Ernest at having to support Billy's mother was intensifying. Feeling ostracized by the publishing world on the one hand and guilty over his mother's situation on the other, Billy—now aged twenty-three—asked his uncle to lend him five hundred pounds for the trip to America. With the understanding that once he got established, Billy would repay his uncle (at six per cent interest) and send for his mother, Uncle Ernest agreed; and Billy booked first-class passage to New York on the *S.S. Merion*, departing from Liverpool on 10 July. All that remained now was a visit to Sussex so Billy could bid a personal farewell to Sherlock Holmes much as Billy had done seven years before when he'd come to Queen Anne Street prior to leaving for the Continent.

And so it was that on the last Sunday morning in April 1912, Billy and I found ourselves at Victoria Station in preparation for the journey to Holmes' retirement cottage. Although I had donned my casual tweeds for the weekend excursion, it was obvious that Billy, dressed in a blue-chalk-striped flannel suit, cut no doubt by a West End tailor, was bidding his farewells in style. A straw boater, perched on his head at a rakish angle, sported an old school-tie band. With a gloved hand, he held his silver-headed walking stick, which happily, since all of Billy's injuries had long since healed, had returned to its rightful role as a simple statement of fashion.

We greeted each other enthusiastically on the concourse, and soon we were settled in a railway carriage clattering along the tracks to Eastbourne. Although I had travelled by railway to the Sussex Downs many times after Holmes had moved there, I never tired of the trip. Especially exhilarating was the sense of seeing something anew whenever I was accompanied by a companion like Billy, who'd never made the journey before. Once the grimy buildings and soot-covered chimneys of London were behind us, Billy and I could marvel at the spring landscape that surrounded the rails. Soon the rolling hills—some covered in the yellows, blues, and purples of wildflowers, other sprinkled with white sheep and mottled cattle—gave way to thickets and forests, which in turn gave way to the chalky earth and ultimately to the white cliffs overlooking the English Channel.

With a final shrill whistle, the railway deposited us at Eastbourne. An omnibus pulled by two weary horses slowly transported us to the village of Fulworth. From there, we made our way by dogcart the few more miles to Holmes' cottage.

As I have written elsewhere, the welcoming puffs of smoke that emanate from the small red chimney atop Holmes' little house near the sea promise comfortable respite to the weary visitor. Equally promising is the knowledge that Holmes keeps his beehives well away from his domicile. But most comforting of all is the reassuring crunch one's boots make while walking along the gravel path to Holmes' entrance; the crunch signals the end of the journey—it announces that the traveller has actually arrived.

Although Mrs. Hudson enveloped us both in hugs as soon as she opened the door, she was especially pleased to see Billy. After all, it was she who, having first taken in the lad as a novice, had transformed him into so disciplined a pageboy. With great scrutiny she eyed him up and down. "Aren't you cutting quite the caper, then?" she teased. At the same time, she brushed some dirt from the dogcart off his sleeve.

Billy offered a non-committing shrug, but Mrs. Hudson hugged him again.

"So serious, Billy," she said. "But then you always were one to ponder matters deeply."

In response, he took off the straw hat, straightened some dark strands of his hair that had gone astray, and broke into a broad grin.

"Oh, those eyes," she said, "those Irish eyes."

It was easy to see that Mrs. Hudson, even at her age, was still completely charmed by Billy's handsome face and inviting smile.

I have previously offered details of Holmes' cottage—the numerous books in his library that sagged the shelves with their weight, the desultory volumes of science and law strewn on various chairs or tables, the cuttings from recent newspapers and magazines waiting to be filed, the scientific detritus like the Petri dishes and test tubes scattered hither and yon. In short, his digs in Sussex had much the same appearance as our old rooms in Baker Street.

After luncheon, a magnificent rack of lamb prepared with mint jelly by Mrs. Hudson, we adjourned to Holmes' sitting room for port and smokes. Although Holmes contented himself with his familiar briar, he offered Billy and me a choice of rich cigars that he kept in the same coalscuttle he'd used to similar purpose at Baker Street.

We puffed away silently for a few minutes. Finally, through a haze of blue smoke, Holmes said, "So, Billy, tell me your thoughts. I've heard the explanation from Watson, but in your own words, why this escape from England?"

Billy coughed once or twice; he really was more comfortable with a lighter tobacco. As he put it, gin and cigarettes were his chosen *métier*.

He coughed again and, before addressing Holmes' question, cleared the air with a wave of his hand. "I've been blackballed, Mr. Holmes," he said. "That swine Steynwood has had it in for me ever since he learned I wanted to publish the true account of what happened to his daughter—not to mention what happened to the other poor souls who met their deaths in connection with the original murder."

"And you're certain," Holmes said, "that all this resistance you're encountering is not simply because—you'll forgive me—your written work doesn't meet the standards the literary market demands?"

"Ridiculous," he scoffed, his voice growing stronger as the smoke dissipated. "I'll admit I got off to a miserable start with *The Express*, but *The Alleynian* has always welcomed my contributions as have *The Gazette* and *The Academy*. In fact, *The Gazette* published my poem, 'Time Shall Not Die,' just last week. And this coming June, they're still planning to run a couple of my articles—an essay and some book reviews, that we had earlier agreed upon. But they've told me not to submit anything more, especially not anything having to do with Sylvia Leonard's murder. I don't care, of course. It is upon that very subject I vow to focus my literary career. If not here in England, then in the States."

"And do you think," Holmes asked, "that you'll have any better luck in America? Lord Steynwood controls quite a few presses there too."

Billy savoured the port. It seemed to agree with him better than did the cigar. "In truth, Mr. Holmes, I'm ready for something new. I don't believe I will ever give up writing, but the recent essays I've been working on lack the flash that I'm searching for. Writing some of those articles, the ones about literary fops and genteel artists in particular, the ones in which I flay pretentious writers like Raphael Sterne, made me feel better. But you and Dr. Watson have exposed me to crime and murder. You've helped me witness a decadent part of human nature that I'd only read about, but never experienced first-hand."

Holmes bowed his head, as if accepting some kind of honour; I could think only of the beating Billy had suffered from one of Moran's hired thugs: *"First-hand," indeed.*

"We've never really discussed it before," Billy continued, "but after you rescued me from my career as Peeping Tom all those years ago, Mr. Holmes, I was forced to confront a side of my nature that I didn't want to think about: my guilt. Our headmaster, Mr. Gilkes, would never admit that any of his boys could harbour such sordid thoughts as I had while staring at that naked model. And every time I saw

Elaine—Mrs. Sterne—it was like looking through that window all over again. I like women, gentlemen. All women. All ages. Those peeks at that nude wench in Dulwich opened up to me a much larger perspective on the rest of the world; the difference between my view through the window of that photography studio and my view through the window on the world is much smaller than I could ever have imagined."

Billy laughed as he reflected on his observations; then he picked up his cigar and resumed smoking. He seemed at peace with his new insights.

The longer I watched him sitting there so complacently, the more I was beginning to understand his psychological development. He was, I realized, sounding more like the emotionally open American he was about to become than like the two traditional Englishmen who were sitting before him and whose tight-lipped judgements he seemed so keen on avoiding.

"I need to let my thoughts evolve," Billy said. "Maybe they'll take me in a new direction. I've got to put all this rotten reality behind. Terrence Leonard and Elaine Sterne tore me up inside. Maybe writing fiction is the answer. I remember reading Mark Twain's *The Prince and the Pauper* when I was at Dulwich. Those mixed identities spoke to me even then. I am both English and American at the same time: two personalities in the same human being. Mark Twain himself embodied this duality; after all, he was both Sam Clemens and Mark Twain. I have no doubt that he could have written my story as well. *He* understood. I'm willing to wager that the freer society in America will suit me better than the rigid code it has taken so many centuries to petrify in England. Even language is affected. Modern English is decaying here; it's become too formal, too rigid. What's more, with all our linguistic pretensions, very few of us—present company excepted, of course—even talk 'good grammar'."

Billy chuckled at his own solecism.

"It's as if all that British formalism in language can do is to produce a criticism of form and manner. In America, I expect more unrestricted opportunities."

Holmes pulled on his pipe. "I am pleased to see how certain you are in your decision," he said. "That should make your leave-taking easier."

"Yes," he agreed. "Not even the beastly news of the *Titanic* can thwart me. I have already vowed to pay my uncle every pound I've borrowed from him. Plus interest. And, as I'm sure Dr. Watson has told you, I'll be sending for my mother once I find a home in the States. She deserves nothing less for all she's done in raising me."

Still close to his mother, I remember thinking. But all that I said was, "There is indeed much to praise in the wisdom of older women." Who could forget all those years ago when Billy's mother would not be put off by Holmes' initial refusal to help find her lost boy?

Billy held up his glass of port. "To older women," he said.

Holmes and I joined him in the salute: "To older women." And we all drank heartily.

"Where do you plan to settle then?" Holmes asked.

Billy shrugged. "Who knows? New York? I'll be arriving there. Chicago? Nebraska? I spent my early years in the Midwest. My mother told me I was conceived in

Wyoming. Maybe that's why I remember liking those wide-open spaces. To be sure, there was always the chance you'd step in a puddle of tobacco that had been spat on one of the wooden walkways, or be haunted by a dead body that had come floating down a muddy river." He smiled. "You see, I was just a child, but I haven't forgotten."

Billy paused as if to reformulate his future. "Then again," he said, "maybe I'll travel farther west. To San Francisco. I'm open to anything. Maybe even Los Angeles."

"Los Angeles?" I scoffed. "After London?"

"Sure," he said. "One city's no worse than any other. Cities are all full of themselves—and empty at the same time."

"To cities," Holmes said, holding up his glass, "full of mean streets and crimes waiting to be solved."

"Mean streets," Billy echoed, "I like that."

And the three of us clinked glasses.

"Just one last thing," Billy said. "You've got to believe me: whatever I end up doing—whatever kind of work I get myself into—one way or another, sooner or later—I'm going to make public what happened to Sylvia Leonard. You can bloody well count on it. I still have my notes. I'm not going to forget. Even if I have to cloak the facts in fiction, I will tell the true story to the world."

"To Truth," Holmes said.

"To Truth," we echoed and clinked glasses again, each of us aware that this was the last drink the three of us would ever have together.

It took but a few minutes for Billy and me to offer our farewells to Holmes and Mrs. Hudson. Then we traced our journey back to Eastbourne and finally to London.

We agreed to separate at Waterloo—I, heading to my home in Queen Anne Street; Billy, to his mother's in Forest Hill. Yet once we returned to London, despite the cool wind blowing at our backs and the shrieks of train whistles punctuating our unspoken thoughts, we stood together for many minutes in the darkness of the deserted railway platform.

At last, the silence between us began to nag. Looking for something—anything—to say, I noted the starless sky barely visible beyond the concourse roof. "Shakespeare calls it 'husbandry in heaven'," I said mindlessly.

"The French call it '*noir*'," he replied.

Then we could delay no longer, and we clasped hands for the last time. As I looked into his deep and defiant eyes, I couldn't help noting the metamorphosis: I may well have journeyed to Sussex earlier that day with the very British "Billy the Page", but it was every bit the American Raymond Chandler to whom I was now bidding this final long good-bye.

THE END

Editor's Afterword

For readers seeking more background on the two major figures featured in Dr. Watson's manuscript, I offer the following suggestions: The cases involving Sherlock Holmes that are most relevant to *The Final Page of Baker Street* are "The Adventure of the Three Students" and "The Adventure of the Mazarin Stone." Both are easily found in comprehensive collections of Watson's work. I would also encourage readers to peruse two articles by G.B. Newton: "Concerning the Authorship of 'The Mazarin Stone'" and "Billy the Page." As Watson implies, it was Newton's pioneering efforts that suggested the true authorship of "The Mazarin Stone." Both of Newton's essays appear in *The Sherlock Holmes Journal*, the former in the Spring 1959 edition, the latter in Summer 1955.

As far as Raymond Chandler is concerned, readers will discover many references in Watson's account of Chandler's early years that made their ways in various forms into Chandler's own writings. The town of Marlow (later Marlowe) and the name Steynwood (Sternwood) are but two examples. Less obvious are fundamental events in Chandler's life that for whatever the reason found expression in his fiction. The nude model that so scarred his adolescence reappears in the guise of Carmen Sternwood in *The Big Sleep*. The tantalizing pendant worn by Mrs. Sterne suggests the Brasher Doubloon in *The*

High Window. Lord Steynwood's home, *Idyllic Vale*, obviously gave rise to the *Idle Valley* of *The Long Goodbye*. Even the compositional advice provided to the young Chandler by Dr. Watson is echoed in Chandler's own list of literary rules, "Twelve Notes on the Mystery Story." But the most significant detail is young Chandler's vow to tell the true story of Terrence Leonard even if required to disguise the tale in fiction. It may have taken Chandler more than forty years to fulfill his pledge; but faithful to his word and character, he published *The Long Goodbye* in 1954, and in its complementary plot arcs involving Terry Lennox and Eileen Ward, we recognize the origins of the actual stories involving Terrence Leonard and Elaine Sterne. Thanks to the benefits of hindsight, we can now also better trace the evolution of Chandler's aesthetics, how the righteous themes of his early romantic poetry and cynical criticism could evolve through his exposure to detective work at Baker Street into the hardboiled tone of his much later fiction.

For further reading about Chandler, I recommend the aforementioned *The Long Embrace* by Judith Freeman, *The Life of Raymond Chandler* by Frank MacShane (a former professor of mine at UC Berkeley), *Raymond Chandler: A Biography* by Tom Hiney, and the recently published *Raymond Chandler: A Life* by Tom Williams. Be advised that all four books were published before the appearance of Watson's manuscript and thus make no reference to it. "A College Boy: Raymond Chandler at Dulwich College, 1900 to 1905," a booklet written by Calista M. Lucy, The Keeper of the Archives at Dulwich, provides brief but fascinating information and photographs of Chandler's early years in England, and

Chandler Before Marlowe, edited by Matthew J. Bruccoli, contains all of Chandler's early short pieces cited by Watson. For contemporaneous background on the Boer War, Arthur Conan Doyle's *The Great Boer War* offers significant resonance.

The best introduction to the mature Raymond Chandler, of course, is his written works (see, for example, the two volumes of novels published by The Library of America and his complete short stories, which appear in *Collected Stories* published by Everyman's Library). There is obviously much that can be learned about Chandler's views of the world from reading his fiction. But only by studying such works in connection with Watson's newly found text can we fully appreciate Chandler's maturation. Watson's account of the early life of Billy the Page reveals many of the social and psychological forces that helped form the writer Billy was to become. The boy in London, who had trouble composing an account of a missing diamond, evolved into one of the most accomplished narrators of murder and mayhem in American literary history. Thanks to Dr. Watson, we now know why.

One final point of interest: In 1903 Charlie Chaplin made his first appearance on the legitimate stage. It should be noted that, featured in William Gillette's production of *Sherlock Holmes*, the young Chaplin played the role of "Billy the Pageboy."

The Final Page of Baker Street

Also from MX Publishing

MX Publishing is the world's largest specialist Sherlock Holmes publisher, with over a hundred titles and fifty authors creating the latest in Sherlock Holmes fiction and non-fiction.

From traditional short stories and novels to travel guides and quiz books, MX Publishing cater for all Holmes fans.

The collection includes leading titles such as *Benedict Cumberbatch In Transition* and *The Norwood Author* which won the 2011 Howlett Award (Sherlock Holmes Book of the Year).

MX Publishing also has one of the largest communities of Holmes fans on Facebook with regular contributions from dozens of authors.

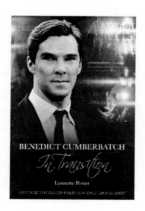

www.mxpublishing.com

Also from MX Publishing

Sherlock Holmes Short Story Collections

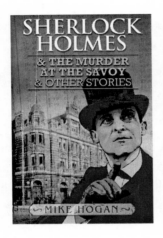 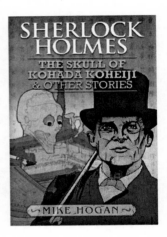

Sherlock Holmes and the Murder at the Savoy

Sherlock Holmes and the Skull of Kohada Koheiji

Look out for the new novel from Mike Hogan
– *The Scottish Question.*

www.mxpublishing.com

Also from MX Publishing

Our bestselling books are our short story collections;

'Lost Stories of Sherlock Holmes' , 'The Outstanding Mysteries of Sherlock Holmes', The Papers of Sherlock Holmes Volume 1 and 2, 'Untold Adventures of Sherlock Holmes' (and the sequel 'Studies in Legacy) and 'Sherlock Holmes in Pursuit', 'The Cotswold Werewolf and Other Stories of Sherlock Holmes' – and many more......

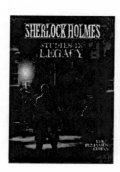

www.mxpublishing.com

Also from MX Publishing

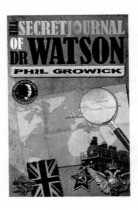

"Phil Growick's, 'The Secret Journal of Dr Watson', is an adventure which takes place in the latter part of Holmes and Watson's lives. They are entrusted by HM Government (although not officially) and the King no less to undertake a rescue mission to save the Romanovs, Russia's Royal family from a grisly end at the hand of the Bolsheviks. There is a wealth of detail in the story but not so much as would detract us from the enjoyment of the story. Espionage, counter-espionage, the ace of spies himself, double-agents, double-crossers...all these flit across the pages in a realistic and exciting way. All the characters are extremely well-drawn and Mr Growick, most importantly, does not falter with a very good ear for Holmesian dialogue indeed. Highly recommended. A five-star effort."
The Baker Street Society

www.mxpublishing.com

Links

MX Publishing are proud to support the Save Undershaw campaign – the campaign to save and restore Sir Arthur Conan Doyle's former home. Undershaw is where he brought Sherlock Holmes back to life, and should be preserved for future generations of Holmes fans.

SaveUndershaw
www.saveundershaw.com

Sherlockology
www.sherlockology.com

MX Publishing
www.mxpublishing.com

You can read more about Sir Arthur Conan Doyle and Undershaw in Alistair Duncan's book (share of royalties to the Undershaw Preservation Trust) – *An Entirely New Country* and in the amazing compilations *Sherlock's Home – The Empty House* and the new book *Two, To One, Be* (all royalties to the Trust).

12/15

Date Due

BRODART, CO.   Cat. No. 23-233   Printed in U.S.A.

CPSIA information can be obtained at www.ICGtesting.com
Printed in the USA
BVOW07s1253020115

381644BV00003B/254/P